D0180304

Jane Austen
ruined
my life

BETH PATTILLO

Guideposts
New York, New York

Jane Austen Ruined My Life

ISBN-13: 978-0-8249-4771-2

Published by Guideposts
16 East 34th Street
New York, New York 10016
www.guideposts.com

Distributed by Ideals Publications
2636 Elm Hill Pike, Suite 120
Nashville, Tennessee 37214

Guideposts and *Ideals* are registered trademarks of Guideposts.

Library of Congress Cataloging-in-Publication Data

Pattillo, Beth.
  Jane Austen ruined my life / Beth Pattillo.
    p. cm.
  ISBN 978-0-8249-4771-2
  1. Women college teachers—Fiction. 2. English teachers—Fiction.
  3. Divorce—Fiction. 4. Austen, Jane, 1775-1817—Appreciation—Fiction.
  5. Americans—England—Fiction. 6. Letters—Fiction. 7. First loves—
  Fiction. I. Title.
  PS3616.A925J36 2009
  813'.6—dc22

                                                    2008043303

Cover design by the DesignWorks Group
Cover art by Corbis
Interior design by Lorie Pagnozzi
Map by Rose Lowry
Typeset by Nancy Tardi

Printed and bound in the United States of America

10 9 8 7 6 5 4 3 2 1

FOR SAM AND MEG, .
WITH ALL MY HEART.

I pulled the well-worn copy of *Pride and Prejudice* from my tote bag and stowed the bag under the seat in front of me. Last time I flew to England, I'd been in first class with Edward, my ex. First class, where they insist that you accept hot towels and champagne along with extra blankets and pillows. Now I was in coach with my knees pressed up against the seat in front of me and the Battery King of Seattle at my left elbow. As it turned out, the only thing worse than having the man snore was having him wake up and start talking to me again.

"Let me get you a drink, sweetheart," he said with all the confidence that wealth gives to a fifty-something man carrying a small child's worth of extra weight.

All my life I had been taught that if you did the right thing, acted with integrity, and didn't make a fool of yourself, not only would Mr. Right come along, but he also would arrive with full financing and a lifetime guarantee of fidelity. I believed this until I was thirty-three years old and found my husband in a compromising position that involved my teaching assistant and our kitchen table. I moved out shortly thereafter, but I let Edward keep the table. How could I have eaten off it after that?

It wasn't quite as easy to run away from Jane Austen, despite the fact that I blamed her for ruining my life. Because while my husband might have killed my belief in marital fidelity, even he couldn't extinguish the hope that Jane had instilled in me from the moment I read those first fateful words:

It is a truth universally acknowledged, that a single man in possession of a good fortune must be in want of a wife.

One sentence of *Pride and Prejudice* and I was hooked like a junkie who had to keep coming back for a fix. So it was no surprise to anyone when I majored in English in college. I went on to do my PhD at the University of Texas, where I met and married Edward. He was a tenured professor. I was a lowly graduate student. But you can't name your daughter Emma and not expect her to go looking for her Mr. Knightley. Edward was older, wiser. He kept me from putting a foot wrong. As it turned out, he kept me from putting a foot right too.

"I'm fine, thanks," I said to the Battery King when he insisted again on that drink. I opened my book, thumbed through the pages to find a good place to start. It was going to be a long night.

What was I doing here, somewhere off the coast of Nova

Scotia at thirty thousand feet? Frankly, I was risking what little resources I had left on a pipe dream. How many other disgraced English professors had cashed in their IRAs and gambled their futures on a stack of old documents that might or might not exist? How many weirdos believed that somewhere in London, a little old lady was sitting on a stash of Jane Austen's letters that had supposedly been burned by her sister, Cassandra?

But when you've lost your husband, your career, and your hope, you might as well bank on the improbable, if not the impossible.

"What are you up to in London?" my seatmate asked. He'd managed to spill most of his manicotti down the front of his shirt, and a good half of his bread roll nestled in the folds of his chin.

"Research," I mumbled as I stuck my nose in my book and hoped he would take the hint. Of course I couldn't be that lucky. Apparently he had all the social skills of one of his batteries.

"I'm meeting with new distributors myself," he said, barely waiting for my answer before launching into a monologue about himself, his business, and his general fabulousness. My good Southern upbringing made me at least pretend to listen, but all I wanted to do was lose myself in the story of Elizabeth and Darcy. I might be out to destroy Jane Austen, but I still needed her like the aforementioned junkie. Just because people buy snake oil doesn't mean they don't need medicine.

"Where are you staying?" The Battery King was not going

to give up his inquisition easily. "I'm at the Dorchester. Maybe we could—"

"I'm staying really far out of the city. In Hampstead. I doubt I'll even come into central London," I said, lying through my teeth. The suburb where my cousin Anne-Elise lived was only twenty or thirty minutes from the center of the city by Underground.

"I know a great little place for—"

"Oh, look. The movie's starting." *Thank heavens.*

I dug into the seat pocket for my headphones and slipped the buds in my ears. God bless whatever filmmaker had just saved me from my seatmate. Watching the movie, though, meant that I couldn't read my book. So instead, I spent the next ninety minutes staring at the monitor above my head while a famous actor blew up buildings and rescued the requisite damsel in four-inch heels, who apparently didn't have the sense God gave a goose. Fortunately, by the time the carnage ended, the Battery King had fallen asleep again. This time, I didn't mind his snoring nearly as much.

❧❧❧❧❧

Eight hours and one long line at customs later, I sighed with gratitude as the Underground train pulled into Hampstead Station. Overnight flights to England came at the price of sheer exhaustion. Even though it was early morning in London, I was ready to stumble into my cousin Anne-Elise's house and flop on the nearest flat surface, but first I had to get there.

I stepped off the train and was swept along in a mad rush to the elevators, suitcase in tow. Hampstead Station was so far beneath the ground that despite the unusual warmth of the late May day, a chill stung the air.

I had thought I was a chic international traveler, packing nothing more than a twenty-one-inch rolling carry-on and a large tote bag. Just the basics. I had a vague idea of picking up some wonderful accessories and maybe a leather jacket or a vintage cashmere sweater at Camden Market or Portobello Road. I had fancied myself a gypsy. Except now I was eyeing the attire of the tony Hampstead residents and feeling the first pangs of regret. My Armani suit, sold on eBay to help finance my plane ticket. My Prada cocktail dress, on consignment at a vintage store to provide some future income. Everything nice that Edward had picked out and paid for, I had sold or left behind in America, window dressing for a life that never really existed.

The elevator lifted us so quickly that my ears popped, then the doors opened, and the human throng poured toward the exit. I fished in the pocket of my jeans for my ticket. Which way was I supposed to put it in the turnstile? I hesitated, and someone took it from my hand, turned it over, and slipped it in the slot.

"Thanks," I mumbled, but my rescuer ignored my words.

The crowd pressed against me, and I gave my little suitcase a hard yank to make sure it followed me through the barrier.

Outside the station, I stood on the corner and watched

the unending lines of cars in all directions. Hampstead was a quaint eighteenth-century village that had been absorbed into London, but it still retained its old-fashioned charm. Storefronts, two and three stories tall, hovered overhead. The High Street was as bustling as the terminal at Gatwick, and the cross street wasn't much better. I searched for a road sign, anything to orient me.

Anne-Elise had said to cross the street and find the little alley passageway that would take me up to Holly Hill. After parading up and down the cross street a few times in front of an estate agent's offices and assorted shops, I finally saw the narrow opening—steep and shaded from the early morning sunshine, a narrow concrete alleyway that climbed upward between brick walls. With a deep breath, I tightened my grip on my suitcase and began my ascent.

Maybe it was the altitude, since Hampstead sits about five hundred feet above the rest of London. Maybe it was all the Krispy Kreme donuts I'd snarfed down since finding my husband *in flagrante delicto* on the kitchen table. But by the time I reached the top of the little passage and then scrambled up the final steep flight of steps, I was out of breath. At the top, I turned back to see how far I'd climbed.

And any remaining breath I had was sucked from my lungs.

High above the treetops and in between the chimneys and the steep-pitched roofs, I could see London spread out in the distance. The British Telecom Tower. The London Eye. A glint of sunlight on the Thames. It was like a Constable painting for the new millennium, complete with golden sunshine and high puffy clouds. Suddenly the city seemed less an icy grand dame and more a magical wash of color and light.

And suddenly I felt less humiliated. There was a tiny hint of optimism. This was my new life. My fresh start. I'd learned from my mistakes. This time would be different. No more illusions about happy endings or divine plans or any of that nonsense.

A new spring in my step, I rolled my suitcase toward number 10 Holly Hill. The Georgian town house was gorgeous, the brick painted a deep blue with white shutters. Its green front door centered it, nestled as it was in a row of terraced beauties, and flowering vines of some sort climbed toward the upper windows.

Anne-Elise's front door was so small, it looked like it had been built for hobbits. Between the cobblestone street and the brass light fixtures on either side of the door, I was hopelessly charmed.

I put the key in the lock and eventually wrestled it open. Nothing a little WD-40 wouldn't cure, I thought, still reveling in my renewed optimism. The door swung wide, and I stepped inside. I found myself in a small foyer. With a sigh of gratitude, I lifted my suitcase over the threshold and closed the door behind me.

That's when I looked up and saw the tall, thin, half-naked man standing in the hallway, clutching a towel around his waist.

Not just any half-naked man, of course. No, a random stranger would have been far more manageable. Instead, it was Adam. Adam, who, until the day I married Edward, had been my best friend in the whole world. Adam, whom I hadn't seen or talked to in almost a decade.

I was certainly seeing him now.

screamed. Even though I knew Adam, knew he wasn't some deranged loony tune who was going to pull a knife and demand either money or my virtue. Or both. But the combination of exhaustion, grief, and surprise pushed me over the edge.

"Hush!" Adam dove at me and clamped a hand over my mouth. His momentum carried us both on a collision course with the front door.

"Umph" was all I could manage as my spine met unyielding wood. That door might be small, but it was certainly sturdy.

"Sorry. But the neighbors . . ." He dropped his hand when he realized it was still covering my mouth. "Sorry. I didn't mean to—"

"What are you doing here?" Was that my voice that sounded so shrill? I paused, swallowed, took a few deep breaths. "How in the world—" And then I stopped. "Oh," I said, the breath whooshing out of me in a stream of understanding. "I forgot. You and Anne-Elise—"

"Used to date," Adam supplied helpfully. "Since you're the one who introduced us, I'm glad you remembered."

I was still leaning against the door, grateful for its solid presence because I'm not sure I could have remained upright otherwise.

"What are you doing here?" I demanded.

"Well, several things. Research, for one. At the British Library."

"Could you please put some clothes on?" I said, careful to keep my eyes above the level of Adam's shoulder.

I'd given some thought over the years to what I would say to him if I ever saw him again, but whatever witty *bon mots* I'd concocted, I couldn't remember any of them now. Adam had made his feelings about my relationship with Edward more than clear, and I'd pretended not to be devastated by his abandonment. And now, after all this time, here he was, with his dark hair and eyes and the same half-knowing, half-mocking grin I used to find so endearing.

He stepped back and frowned. "I wasn't expecting you t—" He broke off abruptly.

I bristled. "I wasn't expecting you either."

"Touché."

"Go put some clothes on," I ordered, and thankfully I heard him pad off down the hallway in his bare feet.

"Don't go anywhere," he called from somewhere down the hallway. The kitchen, I presumed.

Anne-Elise had explained that the small town house her father had bought for her when she moved to London covered three floors. Sitting room and kitchen on the ground floor, and two bedrooms with a bath on each of the two upper floors.

"There's plenty of room for you," she'd blithely assured me over the phone. "Etienne and I spend most of our time in Paris anyway."

Etienne was the latest in a long line of male hearts that Anne-Elise had conquered. The fact that her mother was French had ensured her success in that department. The fact that my mother was a preacher's wife had ensured my lack thereof.

Adam reappeared in the hallway, this time clad in jeans and a polo shirt. His feet were still bare.

"What are you doing here?" he asked.

Well, what did I expect? That he would be leaping for joy any more than I would?

"I was invited," I answered, gritting my teeth. "Where's Anne-Elise anyway?"

"In Paris. Otherwise I would have been wearing clothes," he said, a faint teasing light in his dark eyes. "She's due back in a few days."

"She told me I could use her place while I was here," I said, restating the obvious.

"I assumed so, since you had a key."

Suddenly I was at a loss. I was so tired that any semblance of clear thinking had completely deserted me. Why was Adam here? And why hadn't Anne-Elise told me that he would be?

"Hey, are you okay?" Adam moved toward me as I swayed

to the right. His hand came up to grab my arm and steady me. "You'd better sit down before you fall down." He tugged on my arm, pulling me down the hallway toward the kitchen. "There's a sofa in here. C'mon."

I followed unresisting, although I couldn't seem to uncurl my fingers from the handle of my carry-on. It rattled along behind me.

"Thanks," I said, but that one word cost me most of the energy I had left.

He led me to an overstuffed sofa upholstered in a sunny yellow linen. "Right here," Adam instructed. "Sit. Or better yet, collapse."

I did as instructed. The sofa caught me in its fluffy trap, and I succumbed.

"Do you want some tea?" Adam asked. "You look like you need it."

"When in Rome," I mumbled.

He smiled again, a flash of white against his olive skin, and moved away. Through bleary eyes, I followed his progress across the room, wondering if I was hallucinating.

Anne-Elise's kitchen was something out of an anglophile fantasy. Beamed ceilings, limestone walls that glowed richly in the morning light, an old-fashioned plate dresser filled with blue and white dinnerware. An Aga stove had been retrofitted into the enormous fireplace.

Adam stood there, his back to me, attending to the tea kettle. Between the kitchen area and the sofa where I lay, a well-scrubbed farmhouse table stretched almost the length of the room. I could only be glad that Edward would never see it. The enormity of it would surely inspire him.

"I think I've died and gone to heaven," I said, although I hadn't really meant to give voice to the words inside my head.

"You haven't even tasted my Earl Grey yet," Adam answered.

"This is weird." I sank further into the couch.

Adam looked at me over his shoulder. "Ya think?" He laughed. "You weren't even the one who was caught with his pants down. So to speak."

In my exhaustion, this struck me as hysterically funny. I started to laugh so hard that soon I was shaking. And then, in an instant, the laughter and the shaking turned to full-on tears. I turned my face into the sofa pillows to try and hide my reaction from Adam.

"Hey." He was there, kneeling beside me, one hand on my shoulder. "Hey."

I thought I'd cried all the tears there were to cry in the months since I'd moved out of the home I'd shared with Edward. Clearly, I was wrong.

"I'm sorry," I said, my words muffled by the pillow.

"It's okay. It'll be okay." Adam rubbed his hand between my shoulder blades. I turned my head so that I could see him.

"I'm lying on a borrowed sofa, with no money to speak of, in one of the most expensive cities in the world, and I've just seen my former best friend in a towel. How in the world is that going to turn out okay?"

He really did have the nicest smile. His eyes lit with laughter.

"Well, number one, at least you have a sofa to collapse on, like a heroine out of some romance novel."

"True." I sniffed.

"Two, I'm something of an expert at living in London on the cheap. I'll show you the ropes. How does that sound?"

"Okay, I guess." I waited for him to address my third complaint. Now, though, he was the one who suddenly looked uncomfortable.

"Maybe we could just forget about that third thing," he said, turning slightly away from me.

"I'm sorry," I said, remorse surging inside me to swamp the self-pity. "I'm being a real pain." I pushed myself up to a sitting position. "I didn't mean to bother you."

"You didn't know I was here." He was looking at me again, this time with no discomfort. "Why don't you take a nap?" He glanced at his watch. "I'll wake you up in an hour or two."

"But I'm not supposed to . . . The jet lag thing . . ." By this point, I couldn't even complete my sentences.

"How long are you in London?" he asked.

I sighed. "Not long. A couple of weeks, maybe."

He nodded. "Plenty of time to get over jet lag. For now, just rest." He reached behind me and snagged an afghan draped across the top of the sofa. With a quick snap of his wrists, he unfolded it and spread it over me.

"But—"

He laid a finger across my lips. "Don't argue. Just do it."

All I could do was nod. The last thing I remembered, just

before I closed my eyes, was looking at Adam and wondering if his brown eyes had always been that warm and inviting. And why he kept looking at his watch.

❦❦❦❦❦

When I awoke, the sun was streaming in through the west-facing windows of Anne-Elise's kitchen. Adam was nowhere in sight. Obviously he'd left me to sleep for far longer than the promised hour or two.

I pushed back the afghan and stood up. My head was much clearer, thank goodness, and I no longer felt like I would burst into tears at any moment. A splash of white on the table caught my eye. A note. Adam hadn't completely abandoned me after all.

GONE SHOPPING, it said in block letters. BACK SOON.

Jane Austen would have said that Adam was sadly lacking as a correspondent. I could only hope he'd gone out to get groceries. My stomach was growling so loud, it was probably what had woken me.

The kettle still sat on the Aga, but I had no idea how to use the enormous stove. A bit of searching located the refrigerator, a tiny thing that fit beneath the countertop. I retrieved a bottle of water and twisted off the cap. Before I knew it, I'd downed half the contents without stopping for breath. The water sloshed in my stomach, but at least it quieted the growling.

My carry-on suitcase sat in a corner of the kitchen. Adam must have stowed it there. I crossed to it, laid it on its side, and knelt to retrieve a manila folder from a side pocket. It contained the only evidence to support my outlandish quest—a handful of letters I'd exchanged over the past few months with a Mrs. Gwendolyn Parrot, who claimed to have knowledge of Jane Austen's lost letters. She'd first written me not long after I discovered Edward's betrayal, and those letters had helped to keep my spirits up during the farce of an academic trial I endured. I'd asked Mrs. Parrot if she would be willing to send me photocopies of the letters. Instead, she invited me to visit her in South Kensington, a leafy part of London that was popular with young families and French expatriates.

A sane person, a person whose life hadn't just fallen apart, might have written off her invitation as the lure of a lonely old woman who merely wanted company. But there had been something in the wording of her letters. Again, a vagueness that provided no definite information but somehow called to me. I'd continued the correspondence, hoping for clarification, but I only received a renewal of the invitation to visit.

This last letter had arrived in my mailbox the same day my divorce became final. Somehow the two became intertwined in my mind. I'd gone to the computer and searched for the cheapest airfare to London I could find. An hour later, I'd booked a ticket and written an acceptance to Mrs. Parrot's invitation.

But what did I know for certain, really? I sank into a chair at the enormous pine table and looked, really looked, at Mrs. Parrot's letters. Everywhere hints, but never an outright declaration, as Marianne had said of Willoughby in *Sense and Sensibility*.

The front door slammed. *Adam was back*. Before I could hide the letters, he came through the kitchen doorway heaped with carrier bags and smiling with satisfaction. "Did you get my note?"

"Just saw it." I tried to act nonchalant so as not to draw attention to the folder I was holding. "For an academic, you're remarkably terse." I forced a smile to accompany the words, but I sounded sharp.

He shot me a quizzical look. "Woke up on the wrong side of the sofa, huh?" He plopped the plastic bags on the table. "Sorry it took so long. I ended up taking the bus down to Finchley Road so I could go to Waitrose."

"Huh?" He might as well have been speaking a foreign language.

"Waitrose, the grocery store. A proper supermarket, as they say here." He reached into one of the bags and produced a can of Diet Coke. "Ta-da."

"Bless you," I breathed, restraining myself so I wouldn't dive for the soft drink headfirst.

"What's that?" He'd finally noticed the folder.

"Nothing." I tossed it on the table as if it were of no importance. I reached again for the can of Diet Coke, which he relinquished. "Just some notes."

I was probably being overly paranoid, but those letters were my only hope of restoring my reputation and landing a teaching post again. Adam's kindness since I'd stumbled through the front door had almost made me forget a very important fact. Namely, that I could never confide in him about my outlandish quest. Because he was, in fact, Dr. Adam Clark, full professor of English literature at the University of Virginia, and while his focus was Sir Walter Scott, he was still a scholarly competitor who would also salivate at the prospect of discovering—and publishing—Jane Austen's lost letters.

umber 22 Stanhope Gardens was a Victorian terraced house not far from the Gloucester Road stop in South Kensington. There, elegant, white buildings lined the leafy green Victorian square, which was fenced in for the private use of the residents.

The next morning, as I made my way around the square, I dodged schoolgirls in pin-striped cotton dresses and straw boaters—a far cry from the jeans and T-shirts I'd worn in my childhood. Men were setting off to work in dark suits with monochromatic blue shirts and ties. Harried moms herded their kids with one eye on their watches and another on the traffic. In the midst of all the family bustle, I felt very alone.

I stepped off the pavement into the street to avoid a gaggle of children about to engulf me. This was what I had dreamed of, I thought to myself, the jumble of family life that signified a truly happy ending. A dream that had never been further away than it was at that moment.

By the time I reached number 22, tears were stinging my eyes. I blinked them back and bit my lip, hoping that the pain would distract me from the other ache in the vicinity of my heart. It was one thing to come to terms with the idea of what I had lost. It was quite another to encounter it in the flesh.

With determination, I raised the door knocker, a heavy iron ring clenched in the mouth of a ferocious lion, and rapped three times. And then I waited. And waited. And waited. Maybe Mrs. Gwendolyn Parrot had forgotten our appointment. Or else the whole thing was a hoax, as I'd feared from the beginning.

Behind me, the wave of families on their way to school and work had passed. The muffled drone of traffic from nearby Cromwell Road underscored the peace of the square. Still, no one answered the door. With a sigh, I turned to walk back to the tube station. My adventure was over before it had even begun.

And then the door swung open behind me. I pivoted on one high-heeled pump—a poor choice in footwear, but my best attempt to appear professional—and came face-to-face with Mrs. Parrot.

She was not what I'd been expecting. I'd envisioned a hawkish-looking, spare woman, rather like the silhouettes I'd seen of Jane Austen's mother, with her upright posture and the aristocratic hook in her nose. Instead, Mrs. Parrot looked like a well-upholstered granny who spent her days watching soap operas and eating Cadbury chocolate bars. Her hair was a vivid orange, as if Andy Warhol had been her hairdresser. A pair of glasses dotted with rhinestones hung from a chain around her neck, but she could just as easily have carried them on the ample shelf of her bosom. The fabric of her flowered house-dress would have looked at home on a sofa, and her feet were encased in sturdy black oxfords that had seen better days.

"Miss Grant?"

"Yes. Mrs. Parrot?"

"Sorry to keep you waiting, my dear." It was then I noticed the cane in her right hand. "Not as spry as I once was. Come in, then. Come in. No sense standing around."

"Yes, ma'am" was all I could think to say. Where was the elegant English lady that her correspondence had led me to expect? I'd pictured cashmere, Harris Tweed, and smooth silver hair, not Hyacinth Bucket.

I stepped across the threshold and almost ran into her when she didn't move. She looked me up and down. Clearly she didn't need the glasses to size me up.

"*Hmm*" was all she said. Then she slowly turned and moved into the small foyer.

The black-and-white tile beneath our feet practically sparkled. A brass umbrella stand next to the door was crammed with a wide selection of *brollies*. A curving flight of stairs with a wrought-iron banister rose above a large gilt-framed mirror. All in all, the house was exactly what I'd expected, except for its occupant.

"Just here, in the lounge," she said over her shoulder.

I followed her at her snail's pace. Fortunately, it wasn't far. She opened a door and proceeded into a large sunlit room. Again, it was exactly what I'd expected. Gorgeous white crown molding. A marble fireplace with two wingback chairs drawn up before it. Cushions and tables and lots of cabbage roses on the drapes. Even an assortment of china figurines on the mantelpiece.

Mrs. Parrot reached one of the wingback chairs and carefully lowered herself into it. At her right hand sat a small table that held a tea service and a plate of cookies. Or biscuits, as she no doubt called them. She waved me toward the other chair, and I obeyed.

"I appreciate your inviting me," I began, but she held up a hand to interrupt me.

"Let's dispense with the formalities, dear. At my age, there just isn't time." She smiled to show that her words were not unkindly meant. "You have a purpose for being here. I have a purpose for asking you to come."

I nodded, unsure whether I was supposed to say anything in response.

Mrs. Parrot reached for the teapot and a cup and saucer. "How do you take your tea?"

Apparently there was time for tea, if not for the formalities of polite conversation. "With sugar, please."

Mrs. Parrot poured with the ease of long practice, using a small set of tongs to drop a lump of sugar in my cup. She passed it to me, along with a small silver spoon balanced on the edge of the saucer. She took her own tea with milk.

"Now, then, we can attend to the business at hand." She took a sip from her cup, closed her eyes in enjoyment, then opened them and looked at me with a piercing gaze. "I will share the letters with you . . . if you meet my conditions."

"Conditions?" This was the first I'd heard of conditions. Our correspondence had never hinted at anything like this.

"A series of tasks, really, more than conditions, per se."

"Tasks?"

"So that you may prove yourself worthy."

I glanced over my shoulder. Surely Mrs. Parrot had a hidden camera concealed in the crown molding or behind a vase. "I don't understand."

She sighed and set her cup and saucer on the low table beside her chair. "They never do," she murmured, and I realized she wasn't talking to me.

Since we were the only two people in the room, I grew concerned. What if I'd been wrong? What if she was simply a crazy old lady who wouldn't know one of Jane Austen's letters from a back issue of the *Sunday Times*? What if I had come all that way for nothing?

Mrs. Parrot folded her hands in her lap. "Access to the letters is a privilege, Miss Grant, not a right. You must prove yourself worthy of them."

I set my own cup and saucer down on the table next to me. Clearly the time had come to make as hasty an exit as possible. The tea, which had tasted so lovely only moments before, now swished uncomfortably in my stomach.

"I'm a serious researcher, ma'am. I have a PhD from one of

the most prestigious universities in America. Your letters never said anything about tests or having to prove myself worthy."

"Not tests," she corrected gently. "Tasks. A far different thing."

She was loony. Nuts. Or whatever the equivalent British term was for "off your rocker."

"I don't see the difference." I reached down for my purse, slung it across my shoulder, and prepared to stand up. "You've been very kind to invite me—"

"Whatever you do, protect my children from the coarse and vulgar speculations of others," Mrs. Parrot recited, a strange half smile lighting her face. *"The world may know my words, but it has no such privileges with my heart."*

Mrs. Parrot almost glowed, as if light emanated from just beneath the papery skin of her cheeks. Her words were enough for me to let my purse strap slide off my shoulder and onto my lap.

"What's that from?" It wasn't in any of Austen's known letters or her novels. I could quote them all backward, forward, and upside down.

"One of the letters, my dear. I believe number twenty-eight hundred eighty-five."

"Twenty-eight hundred eighty-five?"

"One of the last ones. Written near the end of her life."

"Twenty-eight hundred eighty-five?" I repeated, stunned. Only one hundred and sixty of Austen's letters were known to exist. I paused, squeezed my eyes shut, and asked the question I knew would seal my fate. "How many letters do you have?"

"Personally?" Mrs. Parrot picked up her teacup again. "About five hundred I should think. Perhaps a few more."

"And the rest?"

"In very good hands, I assure you."

"How many?" Adrenaline and disbelief mangled my question so that it was hardly comprehensible, but Mrs. Parrot understood.

"In total, the official inventory lists almost three thousand letters."

"Official inventory?"

The conversation was growing more fantastic by the minute. No doubt I would soon discover that Mrs. Parrot had recently been released from a mental institution where she'd been hospitalized as a delusional psychotic. I glanced down at my tea cup. It hadn't tasted funny, but . . .

"The integrity of the letters has been well preserved, Miss Grant, I assure you."

Integrity of the letters? Was she kidding?

"You say you have almost three thousand of Jane Austen's letters, hidden away, and you're worried about integrity?" I pushed my purse strap back up on my shoulder. Definitely time to leave Mrs. Parrot alone with her delusions. "I apologize for troubling you—"

"Don't you want to know?" she asked. The vague question hung, suspended, in the air between us.

"Want to know what?"

"The truth."

"About?"

"The truth about Jane Austen, of course."

"Mrs. Parrot—"

She held up one hand. "You've come this far. Why give up so easily now?"

Because you're mad as a March hare, I wanted to say, but I stopped myself. No need to be unkind merely because this sweet, tabby-haired lady was unhinged.

"I really think I'd better—"

"Let me show you one, then." She rose rather unsteadily to her feet. "Perhaps that will convince you."

"Show me one of what?"

"Why, one of Jane Austen's letters, of course."

"You have them here? In your home?"

She laughed. "Not all of them. That would be madness, wouldn't it?"

I stood there, my mouth hanging open, unable to utter a word. Madness? We'd passed that particular stop on the delusional express long ago.

"Come with me." She started off toward the door of the sitting room. Mrs. Parrot moved very slowly. I could only hope that wherever we were going, it wasn't a long distance, or up a flight of stairs.

As she made her way through the door and back into the foyer, her shuffling step gave me plenty of time to study her home. We moved down a long hallway, and I could peer into each room. Every inch of wall space was covered in artwork— oil paintings, watercolors, sketches, pastels, silhouettes. The pictures were framed in a jumble of gilt, chrome, and wood, seemingly without rhyme or reason. Here and there, modern photos and portraits sprang up like weeds in a garden.

A jumble of antique furniture formed a maze of Victorian settees, inlaid tables, and random bric-a-brac. There stood a five-foot-tall replica of the Venus de Milo. Next to it, yet another umbrella stand, this one fashioned from what looked to be an elephant's foot. The sight of it made some of the tea in my stomach leap into my throat.

"You have some very interesting things," I said, more to try to anchor myself to normalcy than in a bid to renew our conversation.

"Treasure is in the eye of the beholder," Mrs. Parrot said. She looked back at me over one slightly hunched shoulder with a smile I could only describe as mysterious. "The value of a thing always depends upon your point of view."

Before I could reply, she pushed open another door. I followed her into the dimly lit room. I couldn't see as clearly here, but there was enough light to outline the jumble of objects fighting for space on the floor and over the walls.

"Let me just find the switch." Mrs. Parrot fumbled around for a moment, and then suddenly the room was illuminated.

"Oh!" I stood there, my mouth agape. Rows and rows of shelves lined the walls, each one crammed with dozens of books. Desks of every size and shape covered almost all of the floor space.

"What in the world—"

"One of our research rooms," she said, giving me a tip of her head to indicate that I should follow her. "Over the years, our mission has expanded."

"Our research room? Our mission?" Mrs. Parrot was merrily leading me down the same road to madness that she had already traveled. "Who do you mean?"

"The Formidables, of course."

"The Formidables?"

I recognized the phrase immediately. Jane Austen's own appellation for herself and her sister, Cassandra, in their later years. As in the formidable maiden aunts who bossed, cajoled, comforted, and cosseted all their relations.

"Cassandra deputized the first of the lot before her death. Fanny Knatchbull was one," she said, referring to Jane's niece and one of her best-known correspondents.

"One of the Formidables." I repeated her words in a monotone, not as a question but as if trying to convince myself that they might be true. A secret society? Devoted to Jane Austen? It was too fantastical to be believed. As an academic, I knew better than to give it a moment's credit. But as a woman . . . a romantic. As my mother's daughter. My heart leaped into my throat.

Of course it wasn't true. It was some elaborate game of make-believe played by elderly ladies with vivid imaginations and too much time on their hands. It couldn't be true. But, oh, how desperately I wanted it to be.

Mrs. Parrot paused next to a set of bookshelves. "You don't believe me?"

"You have to admit, it all sounds a bit far-fetched."

"Most true things do," she replied. She reached up and pulled a heavy volume from the shelf. It wavered in her ancient grasp. I darted forward, caught the book, and helped her lower it to the nearest desk.

"Thank you, dear."

I stepped back, and she opened the cover and leafed through the large gilt-edged pages. "I'm sure I left it in this one . . ."

The mere idea that this obviously senile old lady might actually have one of Jane Austen's undiscovered letters shoved in a book somewhere made my pulse race, both out of excitement and anxiety. "I can help—"

"Here it is." She held up a yellowed piece of paper in triumph, shot me a victorious smile. "Sharp as a tack," she said, pointing to her head with her free hand.

"May I?" I held out my own hand toward the letter. I could see that spidery handwriting covered the sheet. At first glance, the letter certainly looked to be antique, but that was a far cry from actually having been penned by Jane Austen.

"Not so hastily," she said, pulling the letter away from me. "Sit down first."

I resisted the urge to lunge forward and snatch it from her hands. At least she kept it stored in a book, away from the damaging ultraviolet rays.

With great reluctance, I sank into a straight chair pulled up to the nearest desk.

Mrs. Parrot nodded her approval. "Very good. Now, before I show you this, I must swear you to secrecy."

Secrecy? Now she was mentioning secrecy? And then I realized she'd baited her hook quite irresistibly. She wasn't nearly as dotty as she appeared to be. At the moment, I would have promised her my firstborn, not that I was ever going to have one now, for one close peek at the letter in her hand. Even from several feet away, I could tell the handwriting had the right slant and elegance to belong to Jane Austen.

"I will be as discreet as possible," I said, hoping to evade an outright commitment. I should have known that wouldn't work.

"Absolute secrecy," she said again. She glanced around, and then plucked up yet another book from the shelf behind her. She laid it on the desk in front of me. "Swear on this."

"You want me to swear on the Bible?" That was taking things a bit far. And given my current disillusionment with the Almighty . . .

Mrs. Parrot sniffed. "Of course not. People break vows sworn on Scripture all the time. But this? If you're the Austen scholar you claim to be, you'd never desecrate this with a lie." She nudged the book toward me. It was a small leather-bound volume. "Open it," she instructed, and I did. I didn't have to turn any further than the title page to realize what she'd placed in front of me to secure my fealty.

Sense and Sensibility:

A Novel.

In Three Volumes.

By A Lady.

I looked at the date at the bottom of the page. 1811. "This is a first edition." My head swam, and I felt faint.

"Not only a first edition" was Mrs. Parrot's matter-of-fact reply. "One of the author's own inscription. Not that she inscribed it herself," she said quickly when she saw what must have been unadulterated hope on my face. "The publisher wrote that for her. But it was sent at Austen's direction to the recipient. It's only volume one, of course. But I can find the other two if—"

"No, no. That's not necessary."

And it was at that moment that I knew I was going to do it. I was going to swear myself to secrecy. Because if she had this book, one of only a few in existence, then it was not so far-fetched to believe that she was also in possession of at least one of Austen's undiscovered letters.

Later, I would persuade her to release me from my vow. Later, I would win her agreement to publish the text of the unknown letter. Later, I would convince her that no one had a right to keep from the world anything that flowed from Jane Austen's pen. I could already envision the first small steps toward rehabilitating my academic reputation. But at that exact moment, the only thing I knew for sure was that if I wasn't allowed to examine the letter she held in her hand, I would expire on the spot from sheer unbounded curiosity.

efore Jane Austen's sister, Cassandra, died, she was reputed to have destroyed most of the author's letters. Those that she'd saved from destruction were given to various friends and family members, so it took years and years for many of them to be located.

There had always been speculation in the academic world, as well as in circles of Austen's devotees, that other letters would resurface over time, but the expectation had been that these would be occasional rarities. The idea that such an enormous number of letters as Mrs. Parrot claimed might still exist and, what's more, be thoroughly cataloged, boggled my mind. And then Mrs. Parrot gently laid the letter she'd been holding on the desk before me, and my world turned upside down.

True, I was no expert on handwriting or carbon dating or whatever else one needed to verify the authenticity of something like this, but I'd seen enough facsimiles of the real thing to know that this was either the most brilliant forgery ever or it was, be still my heart, the real thing.

A lost letter of Jane Austen.

"You may touch it, my dear," Mrs. Parrot said from her perch at my shoulder.

I reached out and gently traced my finger beneath the signature at the bottom of the page.

J. Austen

I tore my gaze away from the letter and quickly scanned the room. Were the rest of the letters hidden in random books on the numerous shelves as this letter had been? Mrs. Parrot must have seen the surge of literary greed in my eyes, because she gently retrieved the letter from the desk in front of me and tucked it back between the pages of the book.

"Wait—"

She held up a staying hand. "As I was saying earlier, I will be happy to show you more of the letters, provided you accomplish certain tasks that I set for you."

I looked at her to make sure she wasn't joking. Earlier, I'd hoped that she was teasing me, or perhaps testing me. But, no, I could tell from the set of her mouth and the martial gleam in her gray eyes that she was serious.

"What kind of tasks?" I asked, full of trepidation. The little-old-lady persona no longer lulled me into a false sense of security. Shuffling step or no, Mrs. Parrot was a force to be reckoned with.

"They are not difficult, but they will require something of you."

"Such as?"

She smiled as mysteriously as a woman on the wrong side of eighty possibly could. "You shall see."

❧❧❧❧❧

By the time I left Stanhope Gardens, I had sympathy for Alice and her tumble down the rabbit hole. Tucked in my purse was a sealed envelope that I'd sworn not to open until I'd completed my assigned task.

A few minutes later, I ran into Adam on Gloucester Road, across from the Underground station. I was loitering in front of the Starbucks, trying to decide if I could part with almost three pounds sterling for a grande skinny latte. If I'd ever needed caffeine in my life, it was at that moment, but I was keenly aware of the shabby state of my finances. Mrs. Parrot had made no mention of assisting me with the expenses occurred in performing her tasks, and I'd been too proud to bring up the subject. One way or another, I would do what I had to do. I wasn't about to let money stand between me and the discovery of a lifetime.

So there I was, pacing back and forth in front of Starbucks, when I looked up and saw Adam, tall and dark, coming down the sidewalk toward me. My heart started beating double time. Had he followed me? I couldn't let him know about Mrs. Parrot. But, no, he was coming from the opposite direction, and he'd still been sleeping when I left the house that morning. What was he doing so far from Hampstead?

"Emma!" He looked as surprised as I was. "What are you doing here?" He cast a quick glance over his shoulder, which immediately made me suspicious. Adam didn't seem any happier to see me than I was to see him.

"I was . . . I mean . . . I had an appointment. Nothing important."

"Are you picketing Starbucks?" He jerked his head toward the coffee shop.

I shook my head. "Just trying to decide whether to get a latte or not."

And then, it was like he read my mind. I could see the understanding dawn in his eyes. "Let me treat you," he said.

"No, that's—" But he'd already disappeared inside the coffee shop. What else could I do but follow him?

"You don't have to—"

"Grande latte," he said to the barista. "And a tall coffee of the day." He turned back to me. "Unless your usual has changed?"

"No. No, it hasn't." If I hadn't wanted that latte so much, I would have resented his high-handedness.

I waited while he paid. He had no trouble producing the right change. I was still trying to figure out why the ten-pence piece was so enormous compared to the five pence. On the way to South Kensington that morning, I'd resorted to shoving a palm full of change into the face of a newspaper vendor and asking him to just take what he needed.

A few moments later, we had our coffees in hand. When we reemerged onto Gloucester Road, Adam waved toward one of the empty café tables in front of the shop. "Have you got a minute?" he asked.

The envelope burned a hole in my purse, but I kept my

expression from showing my impatience. The sooner I could get moving, the sooner I could accomplish my task and have the right to open the letter. A conscience was very inconvenient at times like this. I wanted to rip the envelope open and be done with it.

"So, you're doing some top-secret research?" he said, prompting me for an answer.

"Look, Adam . . ." And then I stopped. I had no idea how much he knew about what had transpired between Edward and me. Oh, I knew he must have heard about the divorce through the academic grapevine, but I wasn't so sure about the plagiarism charges my teaching assistant had made against me. I didn't know if he knew that Edward had backed her up, or about my subsequent dismissal. It had all been very discreet. The university agreed to let me leave quietly if I didn't kick up a fuss.

"Look," I began again, "I don't mean to be rude—"

"I know about all of it," he said. Again, it was as if he was reading my mind. "Although I certainly have some questions."

I snorted. "Questions? Like, why was I such a blithering idiot? Like, what kind of woman doesn't catch on when her husband is—" I stopped myself. "I'm sorry. You don't want to hear about all this."

"Edward's an academic legend, but he's not God. I think his actions speak for themselves. After all," he looked down into his cup, "it wouldn't be the first time." He lifted his gaze to mine.

With a sudden flash of understanding, I realized what he was saying.

"It's wasn't the first time?"

"That the great Edward Fairchild messed around with a teaching assistant?" He shook his head. "No."

My chest tightened. "Are you saying he cheated on me before?"

Despite all the emotional trauma, it honestly hadn't occurred to me that maybe the kitchen-table girl hadn't been Edward's first dalliance, as Jane Austen would say.

"When we were in grad school—" He broke off. "Never mind."

The latte in my stomach, which had felt so comforting a moment before, turned to sludge. "I had no idea."

"I know."

A new round of humiliation poured through me, lighting a flame in my cheeks. So, everyone had known. Even someone as removed as Adam.

"So it was common knowledge? What happened?"

Adam shrugged. "I'm afraid so." He reached over and laid a hand on my arm. "It's not your fault, Em. The man's a dog. Always has been."

I knew that Adam had disliked Edward, that he felt I'd chosen Edward over him. "Did you know back then? When we were in grad school?"

Adam nodded.

"Why didn't you tell me?"

"Would you have listened?"

I knew the answer to that. "No."

Adam shrugged. "Like I said, it's not your fault. A leopard can't change its spots."

"And no woman deserves to catch her husband laying the table, shall we say?" Even as I said the words, I couldn't stop the smile that played at the corners of my mouth.

Adam looked at me, astonished, and then he started to laugh, a rich, deep laugh that matched his dark hair and eyes.

"Well, that's one way to put it."

And then we were both laughing, a combination of relief and irony that somehow reestablished the bond between us.

I wiped my eyes with a paper napkin I'd grabbed on my way out the coffee-shop door. "I can't believe I came all the way to London only to run into you." The moment the words left my mouth, I realized how rude they sounded. "I'm sorry. I didn't mean it that way."

"Chock full of irony," Adam said. "Austen would have approved."

"Wouldn't she, though?" I grinned from ear to ear.

"Let's do something together tomorrow," Adam said, abruptly changing the subject. "To take your mind off your troubles."

My pulse picked up. Adam might be the only person in the world who could understand the kind of pain Edward had caused me, but I couldn't tell him about the missing letters. "I can't. I have to make a day trip."

"Really? Where?"

I twisted the cardboard band around my cup. "Nowhere special."

"Nowhere special? You came all the way to England so you could go nowhere special?" He polished off the last of his coffee in one swallow. "I'm not buying it, Em."

Em. The old nickname wafted by me, like a favorite but forgotten perfume.

"It's not something I'm ready to talk about. What I'm working on, I mean."

"Okay." He looked at his watch. "I don't mean to pressure you. Look, I've got to get going." He gave me an assessing look. "You sure you're okay?"

"Couldn't be better." When had I gotten so good at lying?

"I don't know what time I'll be home." He stood up, and I did the same.

"We're adults. I don't expect you to keep tabs on me, or vice versa." I forced a smile. "Although maybe I'd better knock extra loud before entering the house, just in case."

Better to tease him than to give in to the tears that suddenly stung my eyes. I'd hoped that England would be an escape from the train wreck that was my life, but Adam's presence ensured that I'd be reminded on a regular basis of how badly I'd erred, of a friendship I'd sacrificed for a sham of a marriage.

"Okay, then. Later."

"Yeah. Later."

We moved toward the pavement. He set off down the street, away from the Underground station, and I wondered again where he was headed. He'd been so busy quizzing me that I'd forgotten to ask him where he was going.

Oh well. What did it matter? Overhead, the sky had grown dark and the first drops of an early summer shower started to fall. I clutched my purse tighter and made a dash for the Underground.

Now all I had to do was figure out how I was going to get to Hampshire, to Steventon, the birthplace of Jane Austen, without Adam or anyone else finding out where I was going.

train ticket to Basingstoke, the closest station to the village of Steventon, was almost fifty dollars. I would have to hire some sort of cab to get me from there to the village itself, another twelve miles or so. And then I would have to pay the cab to wait.

The problem with Jane Austen, I thought as I scribbled my sums on the back of an envelope I'd found on Anne-Elise's desk, was that she'd lived more than half of her life buried in the wilds of Hampshire, about sixty miles southwest of London. It was not exactly a hotbed of public transportation, then or now.

I dropped the pencil, propped my elbows on the desk, and put my head in my hands. I'd been too proud to ask Mrs. Parrot for financial help in completing her tasks. Now I was regretting that pride. To have come so far and to fall short . . . No. I couldn't let that happen.

The front door of Anne-Elise's town house slammed. "I'm home!" Adam called, as if I could have missed his noisy entrance.

"In here," I called from the sitting room just inside the front door. The tiny space strained to hold a desk, two wing-back chairs, a sofa, and a mantelpiece. Underneath it all, a huge Oriental rug stretched from one side of the room to the other. The colors—dark jewel tones of hunter green, ruby, and sapphire—made the space feel even smaller, more intimate.

"Hey." Adam appeared in the doorway. "I'm glad you're here. How do you feel about a picnic?"

I looked at my watch. The afternoon had passed quickly as I'd dithered over how to finance my way to Jane Austen's modest birthplace in Hampshire.

"I could use a break," I said. "Where did you have in mind?" As wary as I was of Adam discovering my secret, I was finding him surprisingly easy to be around even after our years of estrangement.

"Feel like making the trek to Kenwood?"

The former home of the Earl of Iveagh, Kenwood House was the crown jewel of Hampstead Heath, the large park that lay on the edge of the village. I had heard a lot about the beautiful Palladian home. The clean, simple lines and the majestic prospect were considered the ideal of the perfect English country house.

I had wanted to visit it the last time Edward and I were in London, but he'd been presenting a paper at a conference, so instead of visiting Kenwood, I'd sat in a hotel meeting room listening to one of the most boring lectures I'd ever heard in my life. Not that I'd admitted the boring part to myself at the time. Edward's pedantic prosings hadn't been the only thing I'd been in denial about.

"I'd love to." So much for my resolution to avoid Adam so I wouldn't spill my secret.

"I've already got provisions." He held up more plastic grocery bags. The man was a shopping machine, which any woman had to appreciate. "Ham rolls, lemonade, potato chips, and chocolate."

"Sounds perfect."

Twenty minutes later, we set out up the steep slope of Heath Street as it headed north, and then, after crossing near Jack Straw's Castle, we entered Hampstead Heath proper. We skirted the Vale of Health, passing the pond and the gypsy caravans, and then we found ourselves on a sandy trail heading north.

The sun blazed above us, and though I was hot, I was grateful for the warmth. It was a substantial walk, but at last we emerged at the bottom of the park, and I caught my first glimpse of Kenwood House. The pale stone reflected the late-afternoon sunlight, and scores of people were spread across the enormous swath of lawn that dipped down toward the lake on our right.

I was in awe, of course, and I wondered why on earth I hadn't insisted on Edward bringing me here the last time I'd been in London. Had Jane Austen felt this overwhelmed the first time she'd seen Godmersham Park, the palatial home in Kent that her brother Edward had the good fortune to inherit?

I could feel Adam watching me as I drank in the sight of the house.

"They certainly knew how to make an impression, didn't they?" he asked with a teasing smile.

"Could you imagine living in a place like that?" I moved forward, and Adam walked beside me. The path led up in a long curve toward the house. I knew that Kenwood was also a museum. Lord Iveagh, who'd made his fortune with the product that bore his surname of Guinness, had left the house and some rather remarkable paintings—Rembrandt, Turner, Vermeer—to the nation.

"It could be the model for any of Austen's great houses," Adam replied. "Pemberley. Rosings. Mansfield Park."

"Not Mansfield Park," I replied with a shake of my head. "It's too beautiful for that."

Adam shot me a sideways look. "Mansfield Park couldn't be pretty?"

"Austen never really describes it, not the way she does other houses. But I can't imagine a family like the Rushworths living in someplace this elegant. They're too self-centered. Fanny Price was the only one who would have appreciated it."

By this time, we'd climbed the hill and emerged onto a gravel walk that ran parallel to the house. Children scampered by, juggling ice-cream cones, while their parents hustled to keep up with them.

"There's a spot." Adam pointed toward an empty patch of grass not far off the gravel walk. "Let's grab it."

I knew that at the height of summer, there were often concerts on the lawn here and, on occasion, fireworks. Now, though, the lawn—roughly the size of a football field—was full of couples and families enjoying the sunshine and the view. I followed Adam to the spot he'd pointed out. On one side of us, a mother and father were trying to parcel out sandwiches to a pack of whining children. On the other, a couple lay stretched out on a blanket, completely lost in each other. *Great!* I thought with a sigh. How many reminders of my now-single state did I really need?

"So do you think Anne-Elise remembered that she'd invited both of us to use her house at the same time?" I asked as we sank to the grass.

"She'll figure it out at some point." Adam dug into the carrier bag and produced the promised feast. "Organization doesn't seem to be her strong suit."

"No. It never was." I unwrapped the ham roll and took a hefty bite. It was not the most ladylike display, but I couldn't help myself. I'd forgotten to eat lunch, and I was starving.

We munched in companionable silence for a bit. Finally, Adam took a swig of lemonade and then focused his attention on me. "I wish you'd tell me why you're really here." A casual prompt, but it sent my pulse skittering.

"I told you. Research."

He shot me a look of disbelief. "That's pretty vague."

"I just had to . . . get away." I wasn't really lying, but I certainly wasn't telling the truth either. "After the divorce . . . well, I guess I just needed a change of scenery."

Adam handed me a bag of chips. "I knew you and Edward had split up, but I heard about Edward's allegations and your dismissal too."

Heat suffused my cheeks. So he did know after all. I wasn't to be spared that shame either. "I guess everyone knows by now."

My disgrace wouldn't have merited a lot of notice in the academic world on its own, but Edward's position as a tenured holder of an important endowed chair meant that it was news every time he blew his nose.

"What happened?" Adam was frowning, but not at me, really. The expression carved premature lines between the corners of his mouth and his chin.

"I'm sure your source, whoever it was, told you—"

"I want to hear your side of it."

Tears stung my eyes. In all the turmoil of the past few months, Adam was the first person who'd said that to me. Colleagues, friends, enemies—none of them had even thought to question Edward's account, and now here was a man who'd once been my best friend, giving me the opportunity I'd been waiting for to vilify Edward. But if I did that, I had a feeling it wouldn't be nearly as satisfying as I'd always thought it would be.

"My teaching assistant said I plagiarized a paper she'd been working on. Edward backed up her allegations. After that, things moved pretty fast." I stopped and swallowed. "At least they allowed me to finish up the spring semester."

"Why would Edward back up your teaching assistant over his own wife?" His eyebrows arched. "And last I checked, his area was John Milton, not Austen."

Edward fancied himself the greatest living authority on Milton and had convinced most of the academic world of that belief. I was pretty sure he could recite all twelve volumes of *Paradise Lost* from memory.

I shrugged my shoulders at Adam's question. "You mentioned chocolate?" I said, trying to change the subject, but Adam was not as easily led as my colleagues, who had served as judge, jury, and executioner of my scholarly career.

He pulled a Cadbury bar, England's favorite chocolate, out of the bag, but when I reached for it, he moved it out of my grasp. "You didn't answer my question. Why would Edward take your TA's side?"

"I think the fact that he was sleeping with her might have been a factor."

"Oh. That TA."

"Yes. That one."

Adam, having devoured his half of the chocolate bar in little more than one bite, leaned back on his elbows in the grass and stretched his long legs in front of him.

"So, there you were, desperate for some recognition. And you, who've spent your entire career working on Austen, cribbed a paper off a grad student." He smiled at me. "You must have really been desperate."

"I didn't—"

"Of course you didn't," he said. Easily. Simply. Relief, cool and comforting, slid over me like silk. "How did she do it, anyway?" he asked.

"Do what?"

"How did she make it look like you'd plagiarized her?" He smiled. "You know, it's never a good idea to let your mouth hang open when it's full of chocolate."

I shut it with a snap and chewed vigorously before swallowing. "You really do believe me?"

He snorted. "Of course I believe you."

"You're the first one."

He nodded. "I won't be the last, though. Eventually people will catch on."

"It doesn't matter now."

Even if I was exonerated, the plagiarism charge would always hang over my head. There was no innocent-until-proven-guilty in the academic world. A hint of scandal, a whisper, was enough to ruin a career. No, the only way to salvage any part of my reputation was to come up with something so astounding, so breathtakingly amazing that it would make everyone forget about my disgrace and welcome me back into the academic fold with open arms.

"What will you do now?" Adam asked.

I shrugged. "Take up welding?" I said with a watery smile.

I bit my lip so that I wouldn't cry. I was tired of all the tears and the angst. Enough already.

Adam sat up. He reached over and put his hand on my knee. Even through the denim of my jeans, I could feel the warmth of his touch. That was one of the things I'd missed the most about being married—the simple comfort of physical touch, even from a creep like Edward.

"You can't let him win," Adam said. "Believe me, I know from experience."

"When has he ever gotten the best of you?"

Adam had done very well for himself. He'd recently gotten tenure at his university and was considered a leading scholar in his field.

"He hasn't. Not since my dissertation defense, anyway, but only because I've kept him at arm's length." He shot me a rueful look. "Turns out, he's just as big a jerk now as when we were his teaching assistants."

"Why did no one tell me this before I married him?" The words sprang from my lips unheeded.

Adam's face darkened. "You didn't give anyone much of a chance."

"You're right." What was the old saying? Marry in haste, repent at leisure? I'd done both, thinking I'd found my Mr. Knightley. Instead, I'd found my Mr. Nightmare.

"Which brings me back to my original question," Adam said. "No more vague answers. Why are you in London?"

Even if I wanted to, I couldn't tell him now. Mrs. Parrot

had sworn me to secrecy, and if I were to have any chance at all of gaining access to all those tantalizing letters, I would have to keep my word. One whiff of my compromising the Formidables, as she'd called her little cabal, and I'd be out on my ear.

"I've never seen most of the Jane Austen sites," I said, which was true even if it wasn't the truth he was looking for. "I thought it was time."

"Even with your career in the toilet?"

"What a charming way to put it."

"Sorry."

I paused. "You can make it up to me." I hadn't wanted to involve Adam in my business, but maybe I could ask for his assistance without letting him know what I was up to.

"How's that?"

I blushed. "I need your help to get to some of the places."

"Why would you need my help?"

"Anne-Elise said I could use her car, but I can't drive a stick shift." This wasn't entirely untrue. "I need a driver." I had no idea where I was going to get the money for gas, but surely it would be cheaper than train fare and a taxi.

"Where did you want to go?"

"Steventon, for a start."

"I've always heard there's not much there. The rectory where she grew up was torn down a long time ago."

"I know, but I can see her father's church." I couldn't let him know that a page from the parish register, on display in the church, was the main reason for my journey. I couldn't complete the task I'd been given without it. "Besides, it would be great just to see the countryside. I've never been out of London when I've been here before."

Adam gave me a lazy smile. "I think I can play chauffeur. When do you want to go?"

"Tomorrow?" I said, trying to keep my enthusiasm under wraps. As far as Adam knew, it was a casual day trip, not a matter of life and death. Well, my career's life and death, anyway.

"Okay. But let's wait until after morning rush hour."

I would have agreed to just about anything he suggested, as long as it meant reaching my destination.

It wasn't until later, after we'd walked back to Anne-Elise's house and retreated to our separate rooms for the night, that I began to wonder why Adam, after years of estrangement, was being so agreeable. Why he was so willing to drive me to Hampshire. Why had he been in South Kensington that morning or, indeed, what kind of research he was doing in London to begin with? I wasn't the only one being vague.

No, I thought, shaking my head where it lay on the pillow. Edward's infidelity had made me suspicious, made me see ulterior motives where there weren't any. I was boxing with shadows. I refused to let Edward's betrayal make me paranoid. If I did that, then I would lose far more than my marriage.

e left for Hampshire the next morning a little after nine o'clock. Thankfully, Adam filled the car with gas, and we set out in my cousin's tiny Ford Fiesta without my having to confess my dire financial straits. Adam had printed off directions from the Internet, so I sank into the passenger seat, at least as much as one can sink into a car that small, and let him direct our journey.

It seemed to take forever to make our way out of Greater London, but finally we were on the motorway and headed southwest.

"How long will it take?" I asked.

"About an hour and a half, if we don't hit any traffic."

How he could drive on the wrong side of the road was beyond me. I was content to watch the scenery as it passed, and Adam was intent enough on his driving not to mind the lack of conversation. I felt like I'd been dropped into a scene from Masterpiece Theatre, everything was so green and pastoral. At length, we exited the motorway and made our way through the thriving town of Basingstoke.

"Lots of corporations are setting up shop here," Adam told me when I commented on the high-rise office buildings springing up like weeds after a rain. "London's so congested, they're trying to get big companies to locate outside the city."

I could guess what Jane Austen would have thought of multinational corporations invading her territory. I was pretty sure she'd have had a thing or two to say about that.

We passed through Basingstoke and turned off a major road onto a little country lane. "Not far now," Adam said. Two wrong turns later, we finally found what we were looking for. At a junction near an open field, Adam made a left and pulled to the side of the road.

"There you go."

"There I go what?" An open field, grassy and green and trimmed with hedges, lay to my right. It sloped upward until it met a woodsy area. An ancient lime tree was the field's only occupant.

"According to the map, that's where the Steventon rectory stood." He swiveled in the seat and pointed up the hill behind us. "And that's where it is now."

"I remember that later occupants finally figured out that building a house at the bottom of a hill might have had something to do with all that rising damp Austen mentioned in her letters," I said, but my attention was on the scene before me. It looked so empty, that field. Pretty, but empty.

"Isn't there a plaque or something? Some kind of marker?" Adam asked.

I shook my head. "Just the tree. According to what I read, her brother planted it when he was the rector here after her father." My chest ached with disappointment. How could the birthplace of one of the greatest English novelists be so completely ignored? "If she'd been a man, there'd be a ten-foot statue," I said between clenched teeth. "Not to mention a pub named after her."

Adam nodded. "Probably. But I kind of like it like this. Only the true believers like you know the importance of the site."

I wasn't convinced. "Would you say the same thing if it were your hero, Sir Walter Scott? Or Shakespeare? Or, God forbid, Milton?"

Adam laughed at my allusion to Edward. Well, at least my sense of humor hadn't totally forsaken me.

"C'mon," Adam said, starting the engine and slipping the car into gear. "Maybe the church is a bit more impressive."

St. Nicholas Church, Steventon, was a surprisingly far distance up the road—more than half a mile, I surmised. The narrow lane obviously didn't see much traffic. Overhead, tree branches met in a thick tangle. I couldn't imagine a tourist coach lumbering up the lane without damaging its roof. A minute or two later down the country lane, and suddenly there it was. My view of the church was partially blocked by a giant yew tree. But then Adam pulled into the small parking area, and I had my first full look at my assigned destination.

"It's charming," I breathed, afraid to speak too loudly lest it disappear like a mirage.

The thirteenth-century building was constructed along simple lines, a basic stone rectangle rising in a Norman arch to a small, square turret topped by a steeple. The yew tree grew close to the left front corner, as if it needed to lend the building its support. A small fence, built to keep tourists' cars at bay, stood between the empty parking area and the gravel walk that wound its way to the front door.

"What if it's not open?" The terrible thought struck me as I scrambled from the car. Stupid, stupid, I scolded myself. Why hadn't I thought of that before?

"Don't panic yet," Adam said.

Easy for him to say. His entire future didn't depend on getting inside that church.

I tried not to run around the fence and up the walk, but I still moved pretty fast. I beat Adam to the door by several yards. With a trembling hand, I reached out, grabbed the handle, and pulled. It was locked.

"No," I wailed. I wanted to beat against the door with my hands, but somehow I restrained myself. I turned to face Adam, my shoulders sinking. "I can't believe it's not open." One way or another, I had to get inside that church. "What do we do now?"

He remained unperturbed, much to my annoyance. "The sign over there said we could contact the rector. Looks like he divides his time among several parishes."

I slumped against the door. "No, it has to be today."

Adam glanced down at my feet. "Too bad there's no mat with a key under it."

His offhand comment sparked a memory. I looked toward the yew tree. "I wonder . . ." I moved toward it. The ancient branches grew almost to the ground. I pushed aside some leafy obstacles and disappeared into the tree's shadow.

"Emma? What are you doing?" I heard Adam call after me.

Underneath the branches, the air was cool and dim, a sanctuary in its own right. I moved closer to the tree's enormous trunk. It was close to four feet across and had split wide open with age. I'd read somewhere that once a yew tree gets that old, it didn't actually need the trunk to survive, and so the trunk decays and becomes hollow. I could certainly identify.

"I wonder if they still hide it here," I said, half to myself and half to Adam who had followed me into the shadowy shelter of the yew. I reached my hand inside the trunk and felt around. A moment later, I found what I was searching for. "Bingo," I breathed and lifted it from its hook.

It was a church key, but far bigger than any key I'd ever seen, nearly a foot long. I let my fingers trace the curves at the top. "It must weigh a ton," Adam said.

"Pretty much." I had remembered, of course, that in Jane Austen's day, the key to the church had been kept in the yew tree so that any parishioner needing to enter the building might do so.

"Do you think it will work?" I asked Adam.

"I doubt they'd still keep it here if they didn't actually use it. How did you know it was here?"

"I read about it somewhere along the way."

He grinned. "So only true Austen devotees would know where to look. Garden variety vandals wouldn't have a clue."

"Yep." I returned his smile, pleased with my success. We made our way back to the church door. I held my breath as I tried to figure out how to work the key. With a little help from Adam, I managed to get it in the lock and turn it.

"Voila!" I said as the door opened. My heart was pounding. We stepped inside the vestibule, and I got my first glimpse of the interior.

I'd spent the past ten years learning everything there was to know about Jane Austen, but nothing I had read in a book or scholarly journal could have prepared me for the wave of emotion that threatened to carry me away as I moved farther into the church. My chest tightened, and I stepped forward to grip the back of the last pew for support.

"Emma?" Adam moved to stand beside me, and his hand cupped my elbow.

I was supposed to be a seasoned academic, an impartial observer and analyst of the object of my study. But short of the home she'd grown up in, here was the place where Austen had spent the most time in the first half of her life. I could envision her there, on one of the front pews, sandwiched between Cassandra and one or the other of her numerous brothers while they fidgeted through their father's sermon. I'd experienced that myself, trading jabs with my older brother on Sunday mornings while my father delivered his message and my mother bribed us with lemon drops to behave.

"The Anglicans loved their whitewash, didn't they?" Adam said. I followed his gaze, over the plain white walls to the wide beams of the ceiling and the gentle rise of the arches that framed the altar. Matching arches formed alcoves on either side. On the front of the wall that divided the nave from the altar, someone had removed the wash, and I could see the faded colors of the decorative painting that had once covered the interior of the church.

"Most people generally do," I quipped, a desperate attempt at humor. Anything to strengthen my knees and help me draw breath.

Cautiously I stepped forward, the stone floor echoing beneath my feet. Halfway down the aisle, a carpet runner began to dampen the sound. I trailed my hand along the pew backs as I went, desperate to touch something, to make it all real.

When I reached the front, I moved to my right. A table, about the size of a small buffet, held a few mementos, chief among them a copy of a page from the parish register, the record book of the church. It was this page, actually, that I'd come to see, per Mrs. Parrot's instructions. It was actually the sample page from the front of the parish register, the record book of baptisms and marriages and funerals kept by the rector, and Jane Austen had filled this page out as a joke when she was a teenager.

Adam appeared at my side and looked over my shoulder at the facsimile of the document.

"What's that?" He studied it for a moment. "Henry Frederick Howard Fitzwilliam of London," he read. "To Jane Austen. An impressive choice for her first marriage. He must have been a baronet at least."

He was kidding, of course. Jane had filled in her own name as the bride, as she'd done with all of the entries she'd made.

"Arthur William Mortimer of Liverpool." I read the second out loud. "A banker, maybe?" I said to Adam with a smile. "He sounds like someone with pots of money."

"I wonder how she got away with it. Isn't this an official record in England?"

"Her father kept the parish register at home," I said absently. "And it was just the sample page. Not an actual entry."

My eyes traced the printed form, which left blank spaces for the names of the bride, the groom, and the witnesses. The youthful Jane had filled these in, but what had been her motivation? Were these names of real men? Or were they merely figments of her imagination, precursors of the heroes she would someday write about?

"There were fewer than three hundred parishioners in her father's day," I continued. "I can't imagine he performed all

that many weddings, not to mention baptisms or funerals. I
doubt he pulled the register out very often."

"How old was she when she did this?"

"Fifteen or sixteen."

I knew the information like the back of my hand, but seeing her actual writing, even a copy, sent a chill down my spine.
Once upon a time, Jane Austen had been a typical teenage girl,
and from her mock entry in the parish register, I could tell two
things. One, that she'd had her own dreams of love and marriage. The first two entries told me that. And, two, it told me
that she'd always had her sense of humor. Her last choice of
husband was proof enough of that, for the third entry merely
read,

Jack Smith to Jane Smith, late Austen.

It wasn't a very impressive name for a husband, and it
didn't hint at wealth or privilege as the two previous ones had.

"The last one must have been for love," Adam said, echoing my thoughts.

"Maybe Jack Smith was her back-up plan," I said, more to
myself than to Adam, but he threw me a curious look.

"Her back-up plan?"

"Doesn't everybody have one? Don't you?"

"You mean somebody I've made a desperate pact with, so
that neither of us ends up alone in our old age?" He rolled his
eyes. "You are such a girl."

"Everybody has a back-up plan," I said, trying to keep the
note of defensiveness out of my voice. "It's not that weird."

"So who's yours?" he asked.

The question hit me like a fist in the solar plexus, because since the day I married Edward, I'd never given my back-up plan another thought, until now.

"I don't . . ." I didn't know what to say. "I mean . . ." But what was there to say? I stepped away from Adam.

"Hey, I'm sorry." His hand was on my shoulder. He turned me toward him. "I wasn't thinking."

"It's no big—" I burst into sobs. Loud, inelegant, snot-inducing sobs.

"Em . . ." He pulled me to him, and I buried my face in his shirt. Of course I didn't have a tissue or a handkerchief or anything. After all I'd been through in the last six months, you would think that I'd have learned to carry some form of tear-mopping device wherever I went. But I hadn't expected to fall apart like this. Not here. Not now. And certainly not in front of Adam.

"I'm sorry." I pushed away from him and did the best I could to wipe my eyes with the back of my hand. "I thought I was past that kind of meltdown."

"It hasn't been that long." He reached into his pocket and produced, of all things, a handkerchief. "Here."

"You're never going to want this back," I said, but I took it from him anyway, turned aside, and made effective—if rather noisy—use of the handkerchief.

"You're probably right," he said in rather dry tones, but I could hear the humor in his voice. "Maybe you'd better keep it."

I took a last swipe at my face and faced him again. "You're being a good sport. Sharing Anne-Elise's house. Feeding me. Driving me all the way down here."

He shook his head. "First, Anne-Elise is your cousin, not mine. I'm just an ex-boyfriend crashing in one of her spare bedrooms. Second, I have to eat, so picking up a bit extra for you isn't exactly donating a kidney."

I laughed at that. "No, but it's still nice of you."

"And third," he said, stepping toward me, "what self-respecting English professor would pass up a chance to venture into darkest Hampshire?"

We were standing close together now, just in front of the wall that divided the nave from the altar. We were standing where all the Steventon brides and grooms had stood for centuries, where Jane had, obviously, one day dreamed of standing herself.

When had she given up that dream? I wondered. Or had she ever? Did she, like me, grow up believing her father's assurance that there was a divine plan leading her somewhere special? Had she died contented with her single state, or did she still hope to find a man worthy of her vow of marriage? This question, once purely academic, now felt intensely private.

"Go to St. Nicholas Church, Steventon," Mrs. Parrot had said, "and study the page from the parish register."

But what was there to study? What else could be learned from the fictitious names of men that Jane had once conjured in a moment of whimsy? Clearly she had dreams of finding someone to love and marry. Was that what Mrs. Parrot wanted me to see? But I'd known that already, before I'd ever set out for Steventon. What was the purpose, then, of this task?

"Are you all right?" Adam was looking at me with a discerning eye. "You're kind of pale."

"Maybe I should sit down for a minute." I stepped back and moved to the nearest pew. I slid into it and sank gratefully onto its hard surface. "I think I'm still jet-lagged." It was a better excuse than the truth—that now, given the state of my life, my connection to Jane Austen had become too intimate. "I'll just sit here for a minute. If you want to go look around the churchyard or something . . ."

"Are you sure?"

"Yes. I just need a minute alone." Even with my reassurance, he still looked reluctant to leave. "Go." I waved him toward the door.

"I'll be back in a few minutes. Call me if you need me."

"I will."

A moment later, the door shut behind him, and I was left alone in the church. I reached inside my purse and pulled out the envelope Mrs. Parrot had given me. Nothing but my own honor had prevented me from opening it any earlier in violation of our agreement. If I had been in Mrs. Parrot's position, I wasn't sure I would have trusted me that far.

I split the corner of the envelope and ripped open the top. Inside was a piece of white paper. New white paper, like I had at home in my printer tray.

Disappointment ripped through me. She'd told me it was one of the undiscovered letters. Maybe I shouldn't have trusted Mrs. Parrot so easily.

I unfolded the paper and saw then that it was a photocopy. The handwriting, not to mention the signature at the bottom, left little doubt as to the author. My pulse picked up, and I held my breath as I started to read.

STEVENTON, WEDNESDAY, 20 MARCH 1793

My dear Cassandra,

I shall attempt to do justice to your letter, but fear I am sadly lacking in news. Our mother continues in her usual complaints & our father despairs of the lambs...

I scanned the contents, the very sight of the date making my heart race in my chest. The earliest known published letter had been written when she was twenty. This one was dated a full two years prior to that, when Austen was only eighteen. That fact alone made it a stunning find.

...James has written a prologue for our theatrical...

...please do justice to my commission for a petticoat...

...Jack has brought a fillet of beef for our father...

Jack. The name practically leaped from the page. I could recall no one by that name who would have made such a handsome present to the Reverend Mr. Austen.

Jack. But it couldn't be. It was too coincidental. She'd

merely invented a name and written out the marriage in the parish register to amuse her father and shock her mother.

Hadn't she?

Jack. It must have been a coincidence. It had to be. I studied the letter, combing it for another mention of the mystery man, but to no avail.

Mrs. Parrot had sent me to Steventon for a reason. She had instructed me to look at the page from the register and had given me the letter to read. She must have known something I didn't. She'd promised to reveal the truth about Jane Austen, but now I was more confused than ever.

I was still sitting there, clutching the letter in my hands, when Adam returned from his ramble in the church yard.

"Feeling better?" he asked, and I hardly knew how to answer.

"I'm ready to go," I said, stuffing the letter into my purse.

We left the church, carefully locking it behind us and stowing the key in the yew tree once more.

"How about some lunch?" Adam said, and I nodded in agreement.

We drove away from the church, and I glanced back for one last look. *Jack*. That simple name, that one letter, had turned the world upside down. I would always remember the church at Steventon, because I knew, somewhere in my heart, that within its protected confines, my life had been changed.

Now I had to discover exactly how.

CHAPTER

SEVEN

fter dinner back in London—a
classic British fry-up of eggs,
bacon, and toast that Adam had
volunteered to produce—I slipped
out of the house and down the passageway into Hampstead village. I needed some space from Adam and some time to think
about what I'd learned at Steventon.

I walked down Hampstead High Street, unsure of my destination. Even at that hour, the pavement bustled with people
arriving home from work or headed out for dinner or a night
at the pub. Out of habit, I crossed the street and slipped into
Starbucks. Not very British of me, but I was craving the comfort of a skinny latte. I ordered my coffee and looked around
for a table, but the place was packed.

"Would you like to join me?" a voice asked. I turned to my
right and saw a devastatingly attractive man about my own age.
He looked like a California surfer dude who'd been dropped

into the middle of Hampstead, and his American accent made
me smile.

"Oh, I couldn't—"

He waved at the empty chair opposite his. "Come on.
Europeans do it all the time." He winked. "I mean, they share
tables in crowded cafes with strangers." That deep voice, rich
as sin and chocolate combined, weakened my knees.

C'mon, Emma, the voice inside my head said. *Live a little.*
After all, he was very cute. He was American. And he was looking at me as if I were his favorite dessert. I had to admit that
after Edward's betrayal, my ego needed a little stroking.

"I won't bite," he added. "But suit yourself."

His easy nonchalance made the decision for me.

"Thanks." I slipped into the empty chair.

"Barry Morgan," he said.

"Emma Grant," I answered and politely shook his prof-
fered hand.

"So, Emma Grant, what brings you to London?" He lounged
in the rigid, straight-backed chair as if it were my dad's La-Z-Boy.

I froze with my latte halfway to my mouth. "Um . . ." It was
a simple question, but subterfuge was new to me. I was going
to need practice.

"Research," I said. "I'm a college professor." Or was, but
my new friend Barry Morgan didn't need to know that.

His heavenly blue eyes lit up. "Me too. I'm at UC Santa
Barbara." I stifled a laugh. That explained the surfer-dude look.
"Where do you teach, Emma Grant?"

Without batting an eyelash, I gave him the name of my previous employer. He was suitably impressed.

"Very nice. What's your specialty?"

"Jane Austen."

"Hemingway," he responded with a classic bad-boy grin. "Drinking and women and minimalist prose."

He was flirting with me, but I was so out of practice, I didn't even know how to respond except to laugh. He was funny, handsome, intelligent. And he actually wanted to talk to me. *I could get used to this.*

"I'm on sabbatical," he continued, charm flowing as naturally from him as water from a mountain spring. "Just making a stopover in London. I'm headed for Italy, but Sophie wanted to spend some time here first."

"Sophie?" A zing of disappointment shot through me.

He shrugged. "My colleague. She's traveling with me to the conference."

I had to be careful not to squeeze my paper cup too tightly. I didn't want steaming latte pouring out all over my hand.

"What about you?" Barry asked. "Are you traveling with anyone?"

I shook my head. "My . . . my husband and I split up recently." I wondered if telling people would ever get any easier.

Barry leaned forward, lines of concern etched around his mouth. He rested his forearms on the little table. "What happened?"

I didn't want to tell him. Couldn't tell him. Not the truth, anyway. Not the kitchen-table variety.

"We just grew apart," I said, which was true, if you defined adultery as two people growing apart.

He shook his head in dismay. "He's an idiot," he said.

"Yeah, well . . ." I shrugged my shoulders. "*Que será, será.*"

Long before Doris Day, those words had been the motto of the Dukes of Bedford. Edward would have known that. Adam, too, would have caught the reference. Barry just nodded his head as if keeping the beat to a tune I couldn't hear.

"So, how long will you be in London?" he asked.

"I'm not certain. Awhile."

"We should hang out."

I looked at him, unsure whether to be amused or horrified. I had a feeling the unseen Sophie wouldn't be too amenable to my hanging out with Barry, but maybe they really were only friends. His interest and attention were certainly doing wonders for my self-esteem.

"It doesn't sound like you're going to be here that long yourself," I said, trying to steer him away from the subject. "Are you staying in Hampstead?"

He shook his head. "No. The Savoy. We came up here to walk around the Heath, but Sophie got a blister and went back to the hotel."

"I hope she's okay," I said, although I was secretly glad that her departure had given rise to the opportunity to meet him.

He waved a hand. "She's fine. So, have you had dinner?"

I nodded. "I'm afraid so. And I really have to get back."

"You're with someone?" I could see the speculative gleam in his eye.

"Just staying at my cousin's." I wasn't lying, just omitting information.

"Maybe tomorrow? Sophie's having a spa day or something."

"Maybe."

He pulled his cell phone out of his pocket. "What's your number?"

I was too embarrassed to admit that I'd had to relinquish my cell phone after the divorce. Groceries had to come first, and you couldn't eat a cell phone.

"I have an appointment in South Kensington tomorrow," I said instead. "Why don't we meet there? How about the Round Pond in Kensington Gardens? Two o'clock?"

He nodded. "Cool. We can make a plan from there."

I glanced at my watch and pretended to be surprised. "Oh, it's later than I thought. I've got to go."

"Back to the mystery cousin?" He was warming to the challenge already. It had been a long time since I'd been a challenge to anyone, and I had to admit that it felt pretty good.

I stood up, and he did the same. "I'll see you tomorrow," I said.

"Great." He reached out, and we shook hands again. At his touch, a little zing traveled up my arm. "See you tomorrow."

I made my escape as fast as I could. How on earth had I jumped from the frying pan into the fire so quickly? And now

I would have to meet Barry again and spend more time with him, right after receiving my next task from Mrs. Parrot.

Mumbling a few choice imprecations under my breath, I turned uphill and began the climb back to Anne-Elise's town house, wondering when in the world I was ever going to learn.

❧❧❧❧❧

When I walked in the door, I could hear Adam's voice coming from the kitchen. I thought about sneaking upstairs to my bedroom but decided that would look like I was avoiding him. Which I was. So of course I couldn't actually avoid him, or he'd know.

He was on the phone. I stood in the kitchen doorway and cleared my throat to get his attention.

"Yes, ma'am. No, ma'am." Whomever he was talking to, he could barely get a word in edgewise. Then he saw me, and his face sagged with what I could only describe as relief.

"It's your mom." Adam mouthed the words, his hand over the receiver of the handset.

I shook my head. Vigorously. "I'm not here," I whispered. "Tell her I'll call her back."

"Why don't you want to talk to your mom?"

Honestly. Couldn't the man just follow instructions? I made a slashing motion across my throat and jerked my head, indicating the phone.

"You should talk to her," he hissed again. Then he thrust the receiver toward me, and I took it automatically.

How could I explain to him that my mother was the last person in the world I wanted to talk to at that moment? I'd been too embarrassed, too devastated to tell my parents the whole truth about my marriage. "It's just not working out," I'd said to them over the phone, and they'd sounded shocked at first, and then betrayed, as if I'd personally deprived them of the joy of a happy ending for their daughter.

I put the receiver to my ear.

"Emmie, honey, we've been so worried." My mom's voice, familiar and irritating all at once, poured through the phone line. "How are you?"

"Have you been to church?" my dad asked.

"Dad?" Adam hadn't mentioned that my father was on the line as well.

"Not now, Howard," my mom said. "Honey, what do you need? What can we do for you?"

It's strange how even in your thirties, knowing your parents would still bail you out helps you feel better, even if you know you could never take them up on the offer, not without sacrificing every iota of adult independence.

"I'm fine, Mom."

"What about financially?" That was my dad. I could picture them, my mom on the portable handset and my dad in the kitchen, tethered by a fifteen-foot cord to the oldest functioning rotary dial phone in America.

"We can put some money in your account," my mom said. "If you need it."

And there it was. A way out of my difficulties, at least my financial ones. I was so tempted. But I was also a grown-up.

"No, thanks," I said, kicking myself for my stupidity even as the words came out of my mouth. "I'm fine. No problem."

"Well, if you're sure." My mom sounded relieved. "Call us every week, okay? Or e-mail."

"I'll e-mail," I said, seizing on the cheapest option. "Anne-Elise has Internet access here." A fact for which I was profoundly grateful.

"All right, then," my dad said. "Go to church, okay, honey? For me?"

"I'll do my best, Dad," I said, which kept me from adding another lie to my list of sins.

"Honey," my mom said, "why is Adam there? That just seems a little, well, coincidental."

I couldn't have agreed more. "Apparently Anne-Elise doesn't keep very good track of who she invites to visit, so we're sharing. No big deal."

"Still . . ." My dad paused. "I'm not sure I like the idea of you being alone in a house with him."

"Dad, he's an English professor, not Frankenstein's monster." My parents were old-fashioned, to say the least. "Our bedrooms aren't even on the same floor. It's okay, really. And Anne-Elise should be back any day." This wasn't untrue. Just not precisely . . . precise.

Dad harrumphed, which meant he wasn't happy with the situation, but he wasn't going to make a federal case out of it either. Of course, I was a thirty-three-year-old woman who'd been married for years. It was a bit late to start lecturing me about my virtue. Besides, in my whole life, I'd never given them any reason to worry about my morals. It was Edward's morals we should have all been worrying about.

We said our good-byes, and when I hung up the phone, I expected to feel a huge sense of relief. Instead, I was swamped by another surge of loneliness and grief. At some point, I was going to have to tell them the truth about the breakup of my marriage, and how I was now unencumbered by gainful employment. How, in all likelihood, I might be moving in with them again in the near future.

But that would wait. For now, I had plenty to keep me occupied, like figuring out why in the world I had agreed to a rendezvous with Barry the next day. But mostly I needed to decide what in the world I was going to say to Mrs. Parrot, because I wasn't sure that my conjectures about the mysterious Jack Smith were what she'd sent me to Steventon to find.

My head now in as much turmoil as my heart, I bid Adam a quick good-night and climbed the stairs for the refuge of my bed. With any luck, things would look better in the morning.

After all, they could hardly get worse.

ortunately for me, my return trip to Mrs. Parrot's house included an invitation to lunch. I thought of her home, crammed to the eaves with books and furniture and bric-a-brac, and wondered where she possibly had room to store any food. But these days I was grateful for anyone willing to feed me.

"Very well done. You're right on time," she said when she greeted me at the door. This time, she didn't take me into the lounge but led me farther back into the house.

"I hope you don't mind if we don't use the dining room." She ushered me into a small sunlit room barely large enough to hold a table and chairs. "Once upon a time, this was a butler's pantry, but I find it does well for my meals."

The walls, papered in familiar faded cabbage roses, boasted a wealth of early nineteenth-century prints. Fashion plates, mostly, from the ladies' magazines of the time, showing day dresses, evening gowns, riding habits—everything a woman of quality might need. Jane Austen, or more likely her sister, Cassandra, would have studied them and adapted the ideas to their own tastes and means.

"Here. Do sit down. I'll fetch the lunch."

"Please. Let me help."

"No, no. I won't be a minute."

Given her shuffling gait, Mrs. Parrot was going to need more than a minute to bring lunch from the kitchen. I settled in to wait. I'd have much preferred helping her, of course, but my mother had drilled me in the social graces at a young age, and doing as your hostess instructed had been at the top of the list.

The pantry windows looked out on the small garden at the back of the house. The landscape was as jumbled and curious as the inside of the house. No formal parterre here, but rather a mishmash of roses, fruit trees, trellises, and archways. The foliage was lush and vibrant, though. Mrs. Parrot employed an excellent gardener.

The door opened, and Mrs. Parrot reappeared. "Here we are, my dear." She carried the tray with surprising ease, but I still stood up and reached out to take it from her. "Oh, thank you. Just put it there on the table."

The tray contained a plate of sandwiches, two packets of chips much like the ones Adam had furnished for our picnic, and a bottle of sparkling water. I set the tray on the table. Mrs. Parrot settled into her chair, and I did the same.

"So," she said, reaching for a sandwich and placing it on the delicate bone china in front of her, "you've been to Steventon?"

"Yes, ma'am." I hesitated, unsure whether to offer any further answer.

"Here, take your crisps along with that sandwich," she said, referring to the potato chips by their British name. "They're murder on the arteries, but I never can seem to resist."

I hid my smile and did as instructed.

"What did you think of the church?" she asked as she reached for the bottle of sparkling water and poured it into the waiting glasses. "Quaint, isn't it?"

"Yes. And peaceful. I'm glad it's not mobbed by tourists, although I wish the rectory were still there. That empty field was a bit anticlimactic."

She nodded. "Yes, it is, isn't it?" She took a sip of her water. "And the parish register?"

I decided to lay my cards on the table. "I'll be honest, Mrs. Parrot. I'm not exactly sure what you sent me to Steventon to find. But I studied the page from the register, and I read the letter you gave me." I paused. "Is it really authentic?"

Mrs. Parrot smiled. "Of course, dear."

I waited for her to say more, but she merely bit into her sandwich.

"As I said, I'm not sure what you sent me to look for . . ." My words trailed off. "I know I'm supposed to figure it out, but all I could think of was—"

"Was what, dear?"

"Well, after looking at the mock entries in the parish register and then reading the letter, all I could come up with was that
maybe Jack Smith was a real person. Not like the first two."

Mrs. Parrot was nodding. "Very good. Yes, very good. I
knew you were a bright girl."

Since I was on the wrong side of thirty, I should probably
have objected to being called a girl, but I rather liked it.

"So I'm right? Jack Smith was a real person, not a figment
of her imagination?"

"Well, now, that would be telling, wouldn't it?" Mrs. Parrot
popped a crisp into her mouth and munched away happily.

"There's nothing wrong with telling, is there?" I wasn't
above begging if it came down to it.

Mrs. Parrot patted her mouth daintily with a cloth napkin.
"Where would the fun be in that, my dear? No, no. Patience is
the order of the day. All will be revealed in time."

Was she playing me? The thought popped into my head,
and I couldn't immediately quash it. I really had no proof of
her claims, other than my own unsubstantiated belief in the
authenticity of the letter she'd given me. Maybe I was only
seeing what I wanted to see.

"So, did I pass the first test?"

She sighed and laid her napkin on the table. "A task, dear. A
task. And, yes, I would say you completed it quite satisfactorily."
She paused. "I'm surprised, if you're an Austen scholar, that you've
never been to Steventon before. Is this your first visit to England?"

I shook my head. "No."

I didn't elaborate. I was beginning to see how my answer to the question looked from other people's points of view. I'd been to England several times but never for my own purposes. Always for Edward's. Funny how when I'd been in the midst of my marriage, I really hadn't had a very good perspective on it.

"*Hmm*" was all Mrs. Parrot said. "Well, then, it's time to set you about your second task."

"But what about Jack Smith? Am I right? Was he real?"

Mrs. Parrot's eyes twinkled. "My dear, as I said, that would be telling." She stood up and crossed to the sideboard behind me. "Your next task requires less in the way of traveling. In fact, you can complete it this afternoon if you like."

I suppressed a sigh of relief. No travel expenses for the moment, thank heavens. "What is it?"

"A trip to Hatchards, my dear. On Piccadilly. Do you know it?"

"The bookshop?" It was where Jane Austen had been reputed to buy books when she visited London.

"Yes. It's owned by that chain Waterstone's now, but at least they've kept it intact."

"What do I do there?"

"Why, buy a copy of a Jane Austen novel, of course." She smiled, her face lit with good humor. "*Emma*, to be particular. And then you must read it."

"I've read it. Believe me." That one, more than any of her others, had put me on the path to my recent destruction.

"No, my dear, I don't mean merely enjoy it. I mean for you to read it with a careful eye." She paused and looked at me intently. "And when you have finished"—she handed me the envelope she'd taken from the sideboard—"you may open this."

My heartbeat picked up its pace. Another letter.

"But first," she said, "I'll need you to return the one I gave you before."

I'd known this moment was coming and dreaded it. I'd followed her instructions faithfully. I'd resisted the enormous temptation to photocopy it or transcribe it for myself, because I was sure that when Mrs. Parrot swore me to secrecy, it meant not doing anything other than reading the letters with my own eyes. Why I felt so honor-bound to that promise, I had no idea, except that somehow Mrs. Parrot seemed to belong to another time, an older time, when a person's word had meant a great deal, and breaking it had been a cardinal sin.

I reached into my purse and retrieved the envelope. "Here it is."

Mrs. Parrot took it from me without pausing to look inside. I was flattered at her faith in me. I would never have been so trusting.

"Excellent." She sat back down in her chair. "Now we shall finish our lunch. Thank goodness it's only sandwiches. If I'd given you hot food, it would be cold as a stone by now."

I suppressed a smile. She was certainly quirky. But still, for some reason, I believed she was telling me the truth. Or at least

I believed that *she* believed the letters were authentic. Time would tell.

In the meantime, I had a sandwich to finish. And then a roguish Hemingway professor to meet in Kensington Gardens at the Round Pond. Followed by a trip to Hatchards on Piccadilly. And then, with any luck, a long, uninterrupted indulgence with a brand-spanking-new copy of *Emma*.

❦❦❦❦

The unseasonably warm weather had brought Londoners out to the park in droves. I'd hoped to find a spot on one of the benches circling the pond in the heart of Kensington Gardens. I could have a brief conversation with Barry and then make my excuses. Despite the zing I'd felt when I'd met him in Hampstead the night before, I was having second thoughts. After what I'd been through, I needed a man in my life, even a casual flirtation with a man, like I needed another hole in my head.

The Round Pond sat in the midst of the open space of Kensington Gardens—a strange name, I thought, since it was really a large lawn with paved trails running through it, not a garden like I'd always thought of them. The widest of the paths cut from South Kensington northward across the park to Bayswater Road. The pond lay about equidistant from the two park entrances. In-line skaters, dog walkers, and teenagers chatting on cell phones thronged the path, and since there was no hope of getting a bench, I found an open patch of grass and settled in to wait for Barry.

Sitting there, I felt the tension that had been humming through me for the past six months ease a bit. Maybe my quest wasn't so crazy after all. I'd just spent two hours with Mrs. Parrot, and she seemed perfectly sane, or at least mostly sane. I let myself daydream about the what-ifs. What if I completed all of her tasks satisfactorily . . . What if she let me have access to the letters . . . What if I convinced her to let me publish them . . . I could envision my triumphant return to academia. Not to the university where I'd worked with Edward, but somewhere else. A fresh start. My reputation restored. My integrity no longer questioned.

The only thing was, I realized as I sat there, staring at the ducks in the pond, that what I truly wanted back, I could never regain. I wanted to believe in happy endings again. I wanted to believe that I could trust a man. I wanted to believe there was a hero out there for me, worthy of the title of Darcy or Knightley, Wentworth or Tilney.

"Emma. There you are." I jumped at the sound of Barry's voice. "I thought you stood me up." His long stride carried him swiftly across the grass.

"I'm not exactly hiding," I said, trying to sound lighthearted. "Just a little low to the ground."

Barry plopped down beside me. "I wasn't expecting hordes of people." He leaned back, gave me a long look. "You're upset."

I forced myself to adopt a benign expression. "I'm not. Just thinking."

"About me?" He grinned in a charming boyish way that immediately lightened my heart.

"Sorry, but no." I softened my words with a smile, though.

"I've been thinking about you." His blue eyes really were something. Something that could get me into a lot of trouble.

"How's Sophie?" I asked with false brightness. "What's she up to today?"

He shrugged, not dismissive but clearly not caught up in his colleague's schedule. "Shopping, I guess. I can't convince her there's a big difference between a dollar sign and a pound sign. She doesn't quite get the concept of translating currency values."

"Ouch."

"Exactly." He leaned forward and reached out to take my hand. I let him, mostly because the moment he touched me, I felt that zing again. Straight up my arm and then down my spine.

It had been a long time, I said to myself, trying to rationalize allowing him the liberty. It was just like what had happened with Adam, when he put his hand on my knee during our picnic at Kenwood. I simply needed a little human contact. It didn't mean anything more than that. But then I'd always been good at rationalizing mistakes when it came to men.

"So you're free to travel until classes start in the fall?" he asked.

I really didn't want to answer that question, but I couldn't see how I could avoid it now.

"Actually, I've left the university." No need to give him all the details. "I'm trying to figure out what to do next." I looked toward the pond, studying the ducks and avoiding Barry's eyes.

"Everybody needs a change now and then. What will you do?"

I shrugged. "I have no idea."

His thumb stroked my palm, and I started to regret letting him take my hand. It felt far too good.

"If you could do anything, what would you do?" he asked, looking intently into my eyes.

"Anything?" It had been so long since I'd considered that question.

"Didn't you have a childhood dream? A teenage ambition?"

I looked down at his hand holding mine, and memories flared to life. "Yes. I was going to be a world-famous author." I stopped, gave a rather hollow laugh. "I was forever scribbling away with whatever was handy. Pen, pencil. Crayon."

"And what happened to all your scribblings?" Barry asked.

I couldn't believe he was that interested in my innermost thoughts, but his focused gaze and concerted attention seemed to suggest otherwise.

"My scribblings?" I was always diving for a notebook or a napkin or whatever was handy. "I guess I just grew out of it." Although it was only after I met Edward that I gave up writing entirely. "At some point, you have to realize you're not going to write the Great American Novel."

Or maybe I'd learned to block out my desire to write. So many things changed after I married Edward. He'd somehow guided me into merging my priorities with his. Or, to tell the truth, he'd managed to subsume my priorities under his, and I'd let him. I had thought that was the way it was supposed to work. After all, he was much more established in his career at the time, and I was just starting out.

"So you never wrote that novel?"

"What?" I'd been lost in thought, so it took me a moment to process his question. "Oh, no. It was just a passing fancy." But I knew that I was lying even as I uttered the words.

Once upon a time, I had wanted to be a writer with youthful ferocity, but my parents had pushed me to get a graduate degree so that I could teach on the college level. There was no security in trying to be an author, they'd said. "You should have a back-up plan."

And Edward had shrugged off my ambition when I plucked up the courage to share it with him. "You're a good scholar, Emma. Don't waste your energy chasing some pipe dream."

I'd believed them, of course, Edward and my parents. Why shouldn't I have? Doing the right thing meant doing the safe thing, even if I did have my doubts about my abilities as a scholar. I was good at giving lectures, and I could process and present material so that even the most vacuous undergraduate student could understand the Romantic poets or the importance of Renaissance drama.

I wrote my lectures ahead of time and followed the manuscript closely. That was the best use of my writing ability,
Edward had reminded me time and time again. Until the day
my teaching assistant, his lover, managed to take a paper I'd
written on her laptop, which I borrowed while she was on
vacation, and turned it into evidence that I'd stolen it from her.
She hadn't needed a lot of technical skill to make it look as if
she'd been the original author of the work. And as is so often
the case, my peers had believed what they wanted to believe,
which was that the only reason I'd ever been given a teaching
position at such a prestigious university was because I shared a
bed with Edward.

"You're a special woman, Emma," Barry said now, jerking
me back to the present. While I was lost in thought, he'd somehow edged closer.

"Um, well, that's nice of you to say." I didn't know whether
to shove him away or lean in and let him kiss me. At least the
latter course would take my mind off my troubles, although I
had a feeling I'd regret it later.

"Maybe we're star-crossed lovers," he said with a smile.
"Just like in one of your Austen novels. Destined to meet in this
time and place."

"Austen didn't have any star-crossed lovers," I said, leaning closer. He was attractive, smart, and seemed interested in
me. Why should I resist?

"Maybe she should have," he murmured. Then he leaned
in the final few inches and kissed me.

I hadn't been kissed in a long time. Not really kissed. And to be honest, I hadn't been really and truly kissed by Edward for months before the kitchen-table incident. I had chalked it up to overwork on both our parts. A temporary situation that would resolve itself at some point. It had never occurred to me that he was too busy kissing someone else to pay that kind of attention to me.

"Definitely star-crossed," Barry said after he pulled his lips away from mine.

I was glad he ended the kiss, because I wasn't sure I had the strength to do it. That thought set an alarm bell ringing in my head. Physical intimacy was only a temporary fix, I tried to remind myself, but I wasn't really listening.

"Spend the rest of the day with me," Barry said in a low voice.

How easy, how comforting it would have been to fall back into the familiar pattern of relying on a man to solve my problems. It would also have been very dangerous.

I wanted to give in to his persuasions. I knew I could use him to assuage the wounds to my ego and my psyche that Edward had inflicted, but I would have been doing just that— using him.

"I can't." I knew that I had to get away before he talked me into following my baser instincts. The only thing I had left now was my integrity.

Until you betray Mrs. Parrot and publish those letters, the voice inside my head whispered.

"Barry"—I pulled away—"I've got to go."

"But—"

"I'm very sorry." I stumbled to my feet. Taking up with another man wouldn't make the hurt go away. "I've got to go."

"Emma—" Barry lurched to his feet and followed me as I started walking. "Just give me a chance."

I stopped, turned to face him. "I can't."

"You mean you won't." He ran his fingers through his blond hair in frustration.

I paused. "I can't. I'm sorry."

This time when I turned and walked away, he didn't try to stop me. I resisted the urge to turn around, to see if he was still watching me. I resisted because I wasn't sure I was as strong as I wanted to be, as strong as I needed to be.

At that moment, a vacation romance seemed a lot more tempting than an uncertain future, so I forced myself to keep moving, keep walking, and ignore the familiar pang of loneliness that I was afraid was now permanently, indelibly lodged in the vicinity of my heart.

*T*he warm weather turned decidedly hot as I made my way across Hyde Park, too cheap to spring for another ticket on the Underground even in my flight from Barry. Now I headed east toward my next goal and the completion of Mrs. Parrot's second task.

Through the center of London, the parks connect in links of green from Kensington in the west to Trafalgar Square in the east. I crossed Kensington Gardens into Hyde Park, then through the subterranean passages under Hyde Park Corner until I emerged onto Piccadilly, a five-lane nightmare of taxis, buses, and delivery trucks. Here, I followed the road along the edge of Green Park until I saw the Ritz Hotel looming in front of me in all its chateau-style glory. Not much farther now.

I could feel a blister forming on my heel, but I ignored it. Past the Ritz, and then the Wolseley, an exclusive restaurant where

Edward and I had once taken afternoon tea; past Fortnum and
Mason, grocers to Her Majesty, and then, finally, I saw the sign.

Hatchards

Est. 1797

I felt a frisson of excitement, not unlike the one generated
when Barry laced his fingers through mine. It was the electric
buzz of intimacy and connection, only this wasn't romantic but
deeply personal. The multipaned, bowed windows; the tiled
entry; the brass knobs; the history—they all beckoned to me. I
opened the door and stepped inside.

Dark paneling, floor-to-ceiling shelves, and a large twisting
staircase dominated the small space. Books were everywhere—
on a round table in the midst of the room, piled on the landing of the staircase, tucked into the highest shelves. For all its
modern amenities—the cash registers to my right, the electric
lights, the whir of air conditioning—I didn't think Hatchards
had changed all that much from Jane Austen's day.

"May I help you?" an elderly salesclerk asked.

I couldn't speak. My throat was too tight. I shook my head
and darted through the doorway to my left. The ground floor
was a little warren of nooks and crannies. Travel books here.
Local interest there. New releases and biographies.

I took my time, running my fingers along the spines of
books, stopping to pull a title from the shelf and inspect it. A
sense of well-being flowed through me as I circled the ground
floor. It was better than meditation or a new pair of shoes—
or even chocolate. My life was a disaster, but there were still

books. Lots and lots of books. A refuge. A solace. Each one offering the possibility of a new beginning.

Had Jane felt that way when she came here? She'd apparently not been all that fond of London, but she would have appreciated the riches in a place like this. Her father's library, to which she'd been given free access early on, numbered five hundred volumes. Still, no doubt she'd come here with the same motives as any modern shopper: to pick up the newest best-selling novel, the most promising memoir, perhaps even an improving book of sermons.

The classics lined either side of a small passageway between the two main rooms. I found the A's and perused my choices. All of Austen's novels were now in the public domain, so numerous publishers put out their own editions of her works. I pulled a copy of *Emma* from the shelf and flipped it open. For the last ten years of my life, since I'd begun my graduate studies, I'd made a practice of rereading each of the major novels annually. *Sense and Sensibility. Pride and Prejudice.* Her first two, and in many ways, the most successful. Then *Mansfield Park*, followed by *Emma. Persuasion* and *Northanger Abbey* hadn't been published until after her death at the age of forty-one, but there they all were almost two hundred years later, in their various incarnations, still on the shelves of Hatchards. Still on bookshelves everywhere in the world.

The old dream, the one Barry had resurrected only an hour before on the grass in Kensington Gardens, clawed its way up from the depths where I'd relegated it. I ran my hand over the cover of *Emma*, then reached up to trace the other titles on the shelves. The Brontës. Defoe. Dickens. I had never aspired to be in their league, of course, or in Jane Austen's, but Barry had led me to remember that once upon a time, I'd spent hours writing in notebooks and composition books and legal tablets. What had happened to all of them? I'd kept them in a box for a long time, but where was that box now? I'd started numerous stories, dabbled in poetry, tried my hand at a little memoir, but over time, I'd gotten the message that creating my own work wasn't nearly as important as studying and teaching that of the real writers. The ones who surrounded me now.

Jane Austen's family had encouraged her efforts from an early age. Her father, despite his limited financial means, kept her supplied with writing paper, just as he kept her artistic sister, Cassandra, stocked with drawing supplies. He was the first one to approach a publisher with one of Austen's novels, although nothing ever came of that transaction.

Later, her brother Henry served as what today would be called her literary agent. He was the one, after her death, who saw her final two novels through to publication. And it was clear, from her existing letters, that her family all read her manuscripts more than once and had particular favorites among them. I could envision the Austens in the evening, gathered around the fire while Jane read aloud from her latest efforts. I could not imagine, however, my parents or Edward doing the same with anything I had written.

But wasn't it childish to blame the loss of a dream on other people? I looked down at the copy of *Emma*, ran my fingers over the old–fashioned portrait of some nameless woman who graced the cover. No one had forbidden me to write, or threatened me with abandonment or humiliation if I did. At least, not in so many words. But their wishes for my life, their ideas of what was appropriate for me, had been clear as crystal.

I stood up from my perch beside the classics and made my way to the front of the store, where I parted with some of my precious pounds for the copy of *Emma*. Whatever my dreams had once been, I had only one goal now. I had to complete Mrs. Parrot's tasks. I had to gain access to those letters. I had to publish them and regain whatever I could of my academic reputation. The past was over, just as my relationship with Edward was over.

Sure, old dreams might still tempt me, but that didn't mean I should give in to them. On the contrary, I should fight the allure all the more, be even more determined in my course. There was no way, at this juncture, that I was going to let myself regret any more than I already did, and if I allowed those dreams of being a writer to be reborn, I was afraid that my regrets might finally crush me beyond redemption.

With that thought firmly in mind, I took the small paper sack emblazoned with the Hatchards logo from the salesclerk and headed for the Piccadilly Underground station. The sooner I got back to Anne-Elise's house and began reading *Emma*, the sooner I could attain my goal, and the less likely I would be to fall prey to the allure of old dreams.

⟡⟡⟡⟡⟡

Adam wasn't there when I returned to Hampstead. He'd left another of his terse notes that simply said, *Don't wait up*. I laughed, but it sounded a little hollow. As if I was going to keep watch for his return.

Truly, I was delighted to have the house to myself. I kept telling myself how much I enjoyed the solitude as I made a cup of Earl Grey and settled in on the sofa for a marathon session with *Emma*. I was sure that whatever Mrs. Parrot wanted me to notice, it would be some obscure reference, perhaps even hidden in a scholarly footnote or in the preface by an Oxford professor.

Even though I was determined to expose Jane Austen as a a fraud, to use those lost letters to illuminate the gap between her own painful single state and the fantasy-laced happy endings of her novels, the magic of her writing entrapped me as quickly as it ever had. I was happily reconnecting with the village of Highbury and its principal residents—of whom Emma Woodhouse and her father were the most principal—and I was keenly alert for any subtle clue that Mrs. Parrot had intended.

Harriet Smith was the natural daughter of somebody. The line introduced the young woman whom Emma would take under her wing, give airs far beyond her station, and try to matchmake several times before realizing how badly she'd bungled the whole affair. The character of Harriet Smith was a pretty, sweet, not-too-bright young woman, an illegitimate child of an unknown gentleman who evidently cared enough to pay for her schooling but not enough to make himself known. She was a pupil in the local girls' school.

Harriet Smith. Jack Smith. Was it simply a coincidence? Jane Austen's father had, for a number of years, taken in the sons of respectable gentlemen and schooled them along with his own sons. Through letters and diaries, the identities of a number of them were known, but not all of them. If Jack Smith had been an actual person, and not merely a figment of Jane's teenage imagination, might he have been a student of her father's? Might he have lived at the Steventon rectory, growing up beside young Jane?

The thought sent me diving for the few research books I'd brought with me. I pored over them, trying to piece together a reasonable scenario. And an hour later, I had the beginnings of a theory in place. What if the unknown Jack had been the inspiration for Harriet Smith? Only in this case, the pupil in question was the illegitimate son of a respectable gentleman who had been entrusted to the Reverend Mr. Austen for his education? What if he had lived, read, eaten, played cricket alongside the young Jane? Surely she had fancied herself in love with one or more of her father's pupils from time to time. Any girl in that situation would have.

Don't be stupid. Edward's voice intruded on my thoughts. *You're making this up because you want to find something spectacular. You'll be laughed out of academia.* Except I already had been. Well, not laughed out so much as kicked out. Surely this was the trail Mrs. Parrot had set me on.

I spent the rest of the evening alternating between *Emma* and my research books, and while I could find no means of proving my theory, I couldn't find any means of disproving it either. I hadn't finished the entire novel before my curiosity got the best of me and I reached into my purse for the second envelope that Mrs. Parrot had given me. I couldn't wait any longer. With trembling hands, I opened it and drew out the photocopy I knew awaited me inside.

The letter was written to Cassandra from London in late August of 1797. It began with the usual flowing, almost breathless account of whom Jane had seen and what she had purchased, and then there was a passage that practically leaped out at me from the page.

Have been to Hatchards and fulfilled my commission from Jack. Defoe seems a poor choice for a lieutenant waiting to be at sea—but as he will not be guided by my taste, I had better acquiesce to his.

I scanned the rest of the letter as quickly as I could, but there was no further mention of Lieutenant Smith or the book she'd purchased for him there. My heart raced in my chest. I wanted to jump up and run all the way to South Kensington so I could pound on Mrs. Parrot's door and demand that she stop toying with me.

Was Jack Smith really the love of Jane Austen's life? Buying him a book at Hatchards was not exactly an undying declaration of devotion, and it was clear from Austen's letters that whenever anyone went to London, they performed all manner of errands for friends and neighbors.

But the coincidence . . . It had to be more. I felt it in my bones, even if my head wasn't quite convinced. But as anxious as I was to fly back to Mrs. Parrot's, I had agreed as part of my task to reread the entire novel. If I stayed up all night, I could probably finish it by early the next morning.

With renewed determination, I made myself a second pot of tea and settled back down on the couch to read Jane Austen as I had never read her before.

arrived on Mrs. Parrot's doorstep bright and early the next morning, outdoing even my own expectations of how quickly I could finish the novel. I had heard Adam leave before breakfast, and I had left myself soon after.

"Miss Grant. So soon?" Mrs. Parrot's eyes widened with astonishment.

"You said to come back as soon as I finished *Emma* and read the letter."

She looked at me with suspicion. "In one night?"

"Yes, ma'am." My eyes were bleary, and I felt a little fuzzy-headed, but I had done as she'd directed. I couldn't wait any longer to find out the truth about Jack Smith.

She paused, as if deciding what to do. "Come. Let's take a turn about the garden." She reached to the side, and I saw her slip a large iron key and another of her envelopes into the pocket of her cardigan.

Although the key wasn't nearly as large as the one that had opened the door to the Steventon church, its weight still caused her sweater to sag heavily on one side. I couldn't help but think that for whatever reason, she didn't want me inside the house. That piqued my curiosity. What—or whom—was she hiding? For a moment, I thought it might be Adam, but then I laughed at my own fancy. My dealings with Mrs. Parrot were definitely starting to make me paranoid.

She shut the front door behind us, and I followed her down the steps and across the road to the high iron fence that kept undesirables out of the private garden in the middle of the square. Tall hedges screened the interior from view, but I could hear the sounds of children playing.

"How long have you lived here?" Her particular piece of London real estate had to be worth a fortune, and Mrs. Parrot, in her serviceable skirt and cardigan, didn't exactly strike me as old money.

"I've lived at number 22 since I took over as caretaker," she replied.

Before I could quiz her further, we reached the gate, and she retrieved the key to open it.

"A good twenty years, I should think." She waved me inside. "These days, I don't keep up with the passage of time like I used to."

She shut the gate behind us, and we advanced onto the gravel path.

"Clocks and calendars are for younger people. This"— she lifted a hand to indicate the verdant beauty of the garden— "is timeless."

The beauty of the space distracted me from my questions for her. Instead, I found myself entranced by the carefully land-scaped flower beds that wound between open spaces of green lawn. Elegant wooden benches were placed along the edges of the paths, each bearing a small brass plate. As we passed the first few, I could see that the inscriptions were memorials.

Mrs. Parrot led me to the middle of the garden and motioned toward one of the benches. "Have a seat, my dear."

I perched beside her, on the bench dedicated to one Honoria Wellstone, "from her loving husband, Arthur," and hoped that I could interrogate Mrs. Parrot with some appearance of subtlety.

"I think I've figured out what you've been pointing me toward," I began, but she interrupted me.

"You'd be a fool not to."

Well, so much for my belief in my own perspicacity.

"It's rather obvious, isn't it?" she asked with a gentle smile.

"That Jack Smith was one of her father's pupils and that Jane was in love with him? Yes, it's rather simple." I tried to act nonchalant.

"Oh, there's nothing simple about it, my dear. I said obvi-ous, not simple."

"What do you mean?"

"What have you surmised so far?" She looked at me rather intently.

"I think that Jack Smith was one of those unnamed pupils of Jane's father when she was a teenager, or even earlier. He was the illegitimate son of a gentleman who provided for him but didn't make himself known to Jack. Like Harriet, in *Emma*. That's all I've got so far."

Mrs. Parrot nodded. "You're where you should be, then."

Her words made me uneasy. Was I merely a pawn in some game she was playing? Why was she sharing this with me of all people in the first place?

"Mrs. Parrot, you said you were one of the Formidables. What does that mean?"

She crossed her hands in her lap and studied some birds pecking away at the grass a few yards in front of us. "Normally, that information isn't revealed until you complete your tasks."

"Normally? You do this a lot?"

She paused. "No. Only rarely."

"But . . ." My voice trailed off, because I couldn't articulate my objection. I just felt so . . . in the dark about everything.

She smoothed out a wrinkle in her skirt. "Miss Grant, you seem to be under the impression that we're engaged in some sort of game."

I opened my mouth to interrupt her, but she gave me a look that made me hold my tongue.

"For you to even meet with me means that you have been thoroughly vetted. Your being here is not a matter of whim,

nor is it a passing fancy. This is not a game we are playing."
She looked as grim as if she were informing me of a death in
the family.

"I appreciate your meeting with me—"

"It's not a matter of appreciation, my dear. It's a matter of
trust."

"Trust?"

"You are being given access to some very volatile information. I believe that you will conduct yourself accordingly."

"Why? You barely know me." Guilt settled heavy and low
in my stomach.

"I know more than you might think."

Well, that was unsettling, and it nettled me more than a
little. "Indeed?"

"Don't poker up. I may be old, but I'm not a fool. I wouldn't
allow just anyone to waltz into our midst."

"Our?"

"You asked about the Formidables."

"It's really a group?"

"Of course, dear. Why wouldn't it be?"

Why wouldn't there be a supersecret cadre of women who
had been hiding Jane Austen's letters for almost two hundred
years? Gee, well, where to begin . . .

"How many of you are there?"

"Enough to keep the secret, but not enough to make us
conspicuous."

"But why the secrecy?" My mind spun at the enormity of

the prize they were keeping hidden from the world. Not just from scholars but from Jane Austen's legions of fans.

"Because she requested it."

"She?"

"Jane Austen."

Oh. Well, of course. Suddenly, I felt the uncontrollable urge to giggle. "Mrs. Parrot—"

"She had no wish to be known to the world, not even as the author of her novels. Can you imagine that she would feel any differently about her private correspondence?"

"No, I can't imagine that she would. But many writers have preferred privacy, and after their deaths, their letters and other papers have been shared."

"Yes, well, those were other writers. They were not Jane Austen."

"And the Formidables have kept her secret all this time?"

"Yes. Cassandra organized the group, of course. She enlisted some friends, the occasional niece and great-niece."

I paused, wanting to frame my next words just right. "I suppose I wouldn't be the first to say that what you're telling me is too fantastical to believe."

Mrs. Parrot smiled again, that gentle expression that made her eyes sparkle. "Certainly not. And you won't be the last."

But I would, I thought, with an unexpected jolt. If I followed through with my plan to expose the missing correspondence to the world, I would be the last person to sit like this with Mrs. Parrot, puzzling over the mystery of Jane Austen's lost letters.

The end justifies the means, I reminded myself. The world had a right to know about those documents, to study them and to learn from them. In Jane Austen's day, a gentleman's daughter couldn't lower herself by engaging in trade, even one as removed from the actual sales transactions as a novelist might be. But in modern times, well, things couldn't be more different, could they? Had she lived now, she would have been praised and feted and interviewed and revered, not to mention made quite wealthy by her success.

"So you won't tell me any more about the Formidables?"

Mrs. Parrot eyed me carefully. "I won't. But I will send you to meet another member of our group."

From the pocket of her cardigan, she pulled the envelope. She placed it faceup in my lap. "She lives in Bath, so that is your next assignment. You're to go meet her, at this address." She tapped on the handwriting that sprawled across the face of the envelope. "She will give you the details of your third task."

I looked down.

MISS HESTER GOLIGHTLY

#4 SYDNEY PLACE

BATH

"That's one of the streets where Austen lived when she moved with her parents to Bath."

"Yes, she did live there for a time, but that's purely coincidence."

"I can't believe anything about this is a coincidence."

Mrs. Parrot gave me another one of her smiles. "My dear, you should never fail to believe in the power of coincidence. I'm sure Jane Austen would give you the same counsel."

Having read Austen's novels so many times over, I could only nod in agreement. "Yes, I suppose you're right."

"Now, when shall I tell Miss Golightly to expect you?"

I looked down at the envelope. While I was willing to follow her instructions, the time had come to take on a task of my own, to a do a little research to see if I was indeed being sent off on a series of pointless endeavors or whether there was some method to Mrs. Parrot's madness.

"The day after tomorrow? I have an important errand I need to attend to first."

"More important than this?" Mrs. Parrot's eyebrows arched.

"Not more important," I corrected myself hastily. "Just . . . necessary, I guess I should have said. Necessary for me to complete if I'm to do this next task."

She gave me a thorough looking over. "*Hmm*. Very well, then. I'll tell Miss Golightly to expect you the day after tomorrow."

"Thank you. Any particular time?"

"Late morning, I should think. You'll want to look around the town a bit before you meet with her."

"Yes. Yes, I will." I'd never been to Bath. I had only seen pictures, although I'd read about it extensively in the course of my studies.

"Well, then. That's that." Mrs. Parrot stood, and I did the same. She set off, retracing our steps through the garden. "After you've completed the task, come and see me again."

"Yes, ma'am." We made our way out of the garden, and she carefully locked the gate behind us. I walked her to her door. "Thank you again. I'll see you when I get back."

"Very good, dear." She reached out and set a gnarled hand on my arm. "I knew I'd made the right decision, trusting you." She gave me another of her soft smiles. "It's hard to do that these days. So few people understand what we're about." She dropped her hand and turned to unlock her front door. "Safe journey," she said before disappearing inside.

I stood on the front step for a long moment, filled with guilt and self-loathing. How could I betray such a sweet old lady? An old lady, what's more, who'd taken me into her confidence and put her every trust in me? Even if it all turned out to be a hoax, I was going to feel like an amoeba on a flea on a rat when I exposed Mrs. Parrot to the public.

Think about your future, the little voice inside my head whispered, the voice that sounded a lot like Edward. It was that voice of pride and ambition that he had nurtured during our marriage, the one that had made me set aside my dreams of writing for the prestige of being a tenured professor and a scholar.

"Oh, shut up," I murmured as I jogged down the steps of Mrs. Parrot's town house.

A passing gentleman in a business suit carrying a briefcase and an umbrella gave me a strange look. I ignored him and continued on my way, the third envelope clutched in my suddenly sweaty hand.

CHAPTER ELEVEN

f Mrs. Parrot didn't want to reveal anything more about Jack Smith just yet, I couldn't compel her to do so, but that didn't mean I was willing to let her call all the shots. And it certainly didn't mean I couldn't do some research of my own. The question was where?

The obvious choice was that most prestigious of institutions, the British Library, but it was not a library in the usual sense of the word, where you could just walk in and start browsing the shelves. No, even to look at the regular books meant registering for a pass and then waiting hours, if not days, for the requested materials to be pulled from the hidden stacks. I didn't have that kind of time—not to apply for a pass or to wait for someone to find what I needed.

Clearly I needed someone who had access to the library already, as well as someone with a little clout. And, as it happened, I was sharing a Grade II-listed Georgian town house with just such a person.

Adam.

But how to ask for his help without tipping my hand . . .

"Would you have any interest in seeing the exhibits at the British Library?" I asked in a very casual tone the next morning at breakfast.

I had one day to accomplish my objective before I was due in Bath, so finesse had to bow to more expedient methods.

"I've seen it. It's cool." He was deep into the *Financial Times* and nursing a second cup of coffee.

"Do you want to go with me? See it again?" I made every effort to be nonchalant, but some hint in my tone must have clued him in.

"What's your angle?" He laid down the *Times* and took another sip of his coffee. A smile played around the corners of his mouth.

"Why would I have an angle?"

He laughed. "Nice try, Emma. What do you really want from me?"

Well, so much for trickery, even my mild version of it. Maybe it was a good thing that I couldn't lie very well. On the other hand, maybe if I had been more adept at deceit, I would have picked up on Edward's betrayal much earlier than I did.

"I need to get my hands on some books at the British Library, but I don't have time for the niceties."

He shrugged. "Sure. I can help you with that."

I smiled. "And I actually do want to see the rare-manuscript exhibit."

"It may still take some time to get the books."

I paused. "Well, actually . . ."

"Yes?"

"You do a lot of research there. I was thinking, since they know you, they might, well, expedite things a bit."

Now he was grinning broadly. "So, you don't just want me to get the books for you. You want me to call in some favors and get them ASAP."

"Um, yeah."

He laughed. "Okay, but only because you're so cute when you're trying to be underhanded."

I started to laugh too, and then I froze. I looked at Adam across the scrubbed pine table, and he was looking back at me. And for a moment, I felt the jolt of connection, that combination of shock and awareness that signaled mutual attraction. I jerked and my hand knocked over my coffee cup, spilling hot liquid across my lap.

"Ow!" I leaped up from the table and went running for the sink. I grabbed a tea towel from the countertop and dabbed at my legs.

"Are you okay?" Suddenly Adam was right beside me. I could feel his breath against my cheek. "Did you burn yourself?"

"I'm okay. Really. I'm fine." I sort of hopped to the side to put some much needed distance between us. He smelled like coffee and spicy aftershave. I kept patting the towel against my legs long after it had soaked up the worst of the spill. "So, would you have time to go today?"

Adam gave me a funny look and stepped back toward the table. "You have a bit of an obsession, huh?" And then he shot me a speculative look. "What exactly do you need to research?"

"Just a little tidbit about Jane Austen. Nothing that important."

"Yeah, it's so unimportant that you can't go register for your own pass and wait like a normal person for the books."

Shoot. So much for not setting off his curiosity. "I just need to verify a footnote for a paper I'm finishing up." Yes, I was lying through my teeth, but it was for a worthy cause.

Adam's expression, the lines around his mouth, and the darkening of his eyes clearly communicated that he didn't believe me. "Look, Em, you don't have to give me a full report or tell me anything that would make you uncomfortable."

"But? I can hear that 'but' coming."

"But I need to stay on good terms with the people there. I need to know that whatever you're doing is on the up-and-up."

"Up-and-up?" A shot of cold skated down my spine. "Why would you think—" And then I stopped. "Oh, right. My academic misdeeds."

It shouldn't have hurt so much that Adam might have doubts about my innocence, but it did hurt, tremendously.

"I'm doing legitimate research for a legitimate purpose,"

I said, and it was true, even though I had the childish urge to cross my fingers behind my back.

"All right. I'll help you."

"Really?"

"Really."

Relief, warm and fluid, sped through my veins. "I'll go do an online catalog search and let you know what I need."

With any luck, I could uncover some mention, some corroborating evidence that Jack Smith had actually existed. I stepped toward Adam, the sudden impulse to hug him prompting me before my better judgment brought me to a halt.

"Thanks, Adam. I really appreciate it."

"Sure." But he still looked a little dubious. "I'll have to go with you, you know. But if I can turn on the old charm and get you into the reading room, you'll be in business."

"Thank you." The sincerity in my tone must have convinced him that I wasn't using him for nefarious purposes. I glanced at my watch. "Give me half an hour to figure out which books I need."

"I'll call them when you have your list," Adam said. "I know who to ask."

"You're a peach." This time I did step toward him and reach out to squeeze his arm. Since he had his arms crossed in front of him, I ended up with my hand on his bicep. A very firm bicep, I had to acknowledge. Especially for an English professor.

✣✣✣✣✣

Later that morning, we made our way to the British Library, a straight shot into town on the Northern Line of the Underground. Adam was as good as his word, somehow convincing the powers that be to allow me into the reading room and bringing me the books I'd requested. I spent hours poring through them—out-of-print biographies and critical commentaries on Austen—hoping against hope to find just one mention of a Jack Smith, but my quest proved futile.

By midafternoon, I was bleary-eyed, exhausted, and convinced that Mrs. Parrot really was sending me on a wild-goose chase. Adam sat beside me the whole time, reading. I thought he would look over the top of his book and try to see what I was about, but he kept his eyes glued to the page.

"It's no use," I said, as weary and discouraged now as I'd been upbeat that morning. "I can't find what I'm looking for."

"Maybe another day." Adam tried to sound encouraging, which I appreciated, but I also knew that I was looking for a needle in a haystack. A needle with the disappointingly common name of Jack Smith.

"I'm not sure that what I'm looking for exists," I said, despondent. Had I wasted a precious day for nothing?

Adam returned the books, and we left the reading room together. As we made our way toward the exhibit area for the rare manuscripts, I tried to suppress my frustration. The secret I was pursuing was so potentially volatile that I couldn't ask anyone for help in uncovering it, but, paradoxically, I wasn't likely to uncover it if I couldn't ask for help.

"I didn't realize it would be so dim in here," I said as we entered the gallery that housed the rarest treasures of the British Library.

It was as dim and quiet as an ancient cathedral inside. Glass-fronted cases lined the walls and also formed large islands throughout the L-shaped space. The exhibit wasn't large—maybe the size of several college classrooms joined together—but as I made my way into the area, I realized why it was so quiet, despite the number of visitors. For most people, it contained what amounted to the holiest of relics.

"These are the literary manuscripts," Adam said, guiding me to the left.

I stopped at the first display. The case showed the birth of modern English literature—Beowulf, Sidney, Milton, Dryden. I'd seen my share of rare manuscripts, but somehow, these particular pieces lined up side by side, a breathtaking record of the language and literature I loved, caused my throat to tighten. Small descriptions beside each manuscript gave the briefest of background information.

I moved from one to the next, barely aware of Adam beside me. It was one thing to study the great writers of the English language but another to stand there, looking at their actual work, their handwriting, their literary footprints preserved on the original page.

And then there, at the bottom of the case, sat an antique writing desk—more of a wooden box, really—whose lid could be lifted to use as a writing surface, while paper, ink, nibs, blotters, and other essentials were stored inside.

"That's hers," I said in a whisper. Beside me, I could feel Adam grin.

"Do you feel the need to genuflect?"

I made a face at him. "Until the late nineteen nineties, it was stored in some relative's closet, in a suitcase."

He looked at me in surprise. "You're kidding."

"No. There's no telling what kind of Austen-related items might turn up in the coming years. I'm guessing that the descendants of her nieces and nephews have all sorts of stuff tucked away." Not to mention the stash in the Formidables' possession.

I turned back to the case and studied the items intently. Her writing desk was open, a letter lying across it. A pen and a pair of spectacles rested on top of it, but I could still see the letter quite clearly, and it looked achingly familiar, even compared to the photocopies Mrs. Parrot had given me. If the older lady was deceiving me, then she had the services of a top-rate forger in her arsenal.

"There's a manuscript page there, too," Adam said, pointing to a copy of the *Juvenilia*.

I bit the inside of my cheek so I wouldn't cry. I didn't want to look like a total sap. After all, I was a serious scholar, not a fan, but at the moment, I sure felt like one.

"Who else is here?" I asked, aching to move away, like a worshipper who has stepped too close to the divine.

I couldn't stand there looking at the writing desk any longer. We moved on down the glass-fronted case, and I continued to bask in the glow of such amazing treasures.

"Here's Charlotte Brontë," Adam said, pointing to a handwritten book opened to reveal the last chapter of *Jane Eyre*.

Reader, I married him.

Those haunting words that induced tears in the most hardened heart didn't have to work very hard to reduce me to tears. Adam looked at me oddly, then reached in his pocket and produced yet another handkerchief.

"Thank you." I smiled as I dabbed at my eyes and wiped my cheeks.

"It's overwhelming, isn't it?" Adam said. "Maybe we should go to the café, have a cup of tea."

"That's very British of you." I smiled through my tears. You had to like a guy who was that big an advocate of the British cure-all of a cuppa.

When we had settled in at a table in the modernist café just outside the gallery, Adam wrapped his hands around his paper cup and looked me straight in the eye.

"So, what exactly are you looking for, Emma? Why all the secrecy?"

I had to look away while I struggled for an answer that was neither the truth nor a lie.

"If you're going to ask me for my help, maybe you should trust me, just a little."

I turned back to him and knew that my expression must

have been as bleak as my heart at the moment. "Trust is not my strong suit right now."

Adam winced. "Point taken."

"After Edward—"

Adam held up his hand. "Enough said. But, still, you seem pretty determined to find something. How about this? What if you let me help you, but you don't have to tell me anything you don't want to?"

"I really do need to verify a fact for some research I'm doing," I said, aware that I was starting to repeat myself. Not the best way to enhance one's credibility.

"Seems like a lot of trouble for one fact."

"It's pivotal."

"*Hmm.*" He took a drink of his tea. "So, if you couldn't verify it here, what are you going to do next?"

I could hardly tell him that I planned to head for Bath to meet with an elderly woman who was harboring a goodly portion of Jane Austen's missing letters as part of larger conspiracy of silence. So, instead, I shrugged. "I'm not sure."

"Emma . . ." I could hear the disappointment in his voice. "Do you really think I'm going to fall for that?"

"Fall for what?"

"That helpless female routine. I don't buy it."

"I'm not trying to be some damsel in distress."

"That's obvious."

"It is?" Strangely, his accusation made me feel better instead of worse.

"Well, look at it from my point of view," he said. "You had the good sense to dump Edward, and in spite of some academic . . . *er* . . . difficulties, shall we say, you're here, pursuing research that's important to you. I'd say you're pretty resilient."

Oddly, I hadn't thought of it that way before, but hearing the words come out of Adam's mouth, I started to see my situation in a slightly different light.

"Actually, I do need your help with one more thing today," I said, feeling braver. I wasn't sure whether it was the tea, the sight of Jane Austen's writing desk, or Adam's encouragement. Perhaps it was all three.

"I don't think I can pull any more strings for you here," he said, holding up his hands as if to ward me off. "Even my charm isn't that powerful."

I laughed. "This isn't research. It's more of a . . . commercial transaction."

"I'm afraid to ask what that means."

I reached into my purse and pulled out the small velvet bag I'd stowed there earlier that morning. With trembling fingers, I opened the drawstring and poured the contents into the palm of my hand. My diamond solitaire and the accompanying band of smaller stones sparkled under the light from the modern pendant lamp above our heads.

"Your wedding rings?" Adam said, puzzled.

"I need to pawn them, only I have no idea how that works over here."

Adam looked up, his gaze capturing mine. "Emma—"

"I don't want to discuss it, Adam. I just want to get rid of them. And get as much money for them as I can."

He paused, and I could tell he was considering his words carefully.

"Emma, I can loan you the money. Take some time to think this over."

"I made this decision the day I walked into my kitchen and found—" I stopped myself just in time, shook my head. "I need to get rid of these, Adam. Will you help me? And then I promise to leave you alone."

He smiled. "I don't know if I want you to leave me alone. Life's gotten a lot more interesting since you showed up."

A flush crept across my cheeks, and I had no idea why. Except that maybe I did. A little.

"Look, Em, maybe someday you'll want to pawn your rings or something. But I don't think you're ready today. Not yet."

The most frustrating part was that he was right. In spite of everything that had happened, the thought of turning my rings over to a stranger in exchange for a wad of cash made me ache all over again.

"But—"

"Like I said, I'll loan you the money. You can pay me back whenever . . . well, whenever you can pay me back."

His understanding and his generosity shamed me. He was being far too gracious, considering that he was right about me. I had let our friendship go far too easily once I felt secure with Edward.

"I'm glad Anne-Elise double-booked us," I said. "I've missed you, Adam, and I really appreciate your help."

"No problem," he said. He glanced at his watch. "If you're done with your tea, we might as well get moving."

"Good idea." The longer I sat there, talking with Adam and looking into his eyes, the more vulnerable I began to feel, and vulnerable was the last thing I could afford to be ever again.

With that stern reminder to myself, I followed Adam from the café, out of the library, and into the diesel-fumed air of London.

CHAPTER
TWELVE

It's hard for modern-day people to imagine how lives used to be changed by the receipt of a letter. Today, bad news comes over the phone, in an e-mail, or via a text message. But in Jane Austen's day, important information had to travel by post, and so many historical, life-changing moments still rest upon the page for us to witness.

On the train to Bath, I opened my copy of Jane Austen's letters and looked through the book, searching for any clues about Jack Smith. Surely some inkling of her relationship with him remained, although I was beginning to suspect that Cassandra's caretaking of her sister's legacy had been far more thorough than anyone had dreamed. Certainly some of the existing letters had been edited—usually with the help of a pair of scissors—but the general wisdom had always been that Cassandra was merely excising the more spiteful of her sister's comments or her unladylike references to bodily issues.

My dealings with Mrs. Parrot now led me to believe that Cassandra might have sorted the letters into two categories: those banal enough for public consumption, for bestowing on nieces, nephews, and friends, and those that had been hidden away by the Formidables.

Mentions of Jack Smith had apparently been consigned to the latter category, I realized, as I made my way through the existing letters. That realization gave me hope but also made me even more dependent upon the goodwill of the current Formidables, Mrs. Parrot and the unknown Miss Golightly. I would have to do exactly as they told me, which meant continuing to keep their secret, especially from Adam. I glanced at the seat next to me, where he slept as the train clicked along toward its destination.

I hadn't been able to slip out of the house that morning unnoticed after all. After the British Library intrigue, and after he talked me out of pawning my wedding rings, he'd kept studying me with a speculative gleam in his eye. He was obviously very curious about what I was up to, but at least he had the restraint not to ask any more questions. Instead, he'd invited himself along on my trip to Bath, paid for the train tickets, and now I had to figure out how to ditch him before my appointment with Miss Golightly.

As the train left the environs of the city and made its way into the open landscape of the English countryside, I relaxed. Over the course of the past few weeks, I had begun to feel as if I were playing out a prearranged script. Even though I'd lost my faith in what my father would have called God's plan, somehow things were falling into place. The only problem was, I didn't know if the path I was following was meant to lead me to triumph or doom, and given my recent track record, doom seemed more likely.

The day before, when I'd stopped short of handing over my rings in exchange for a substantial number of pounds sterling, I'd felt as if my actions were part of something much greater than me, as if I were a pawn in a larger game. I should have been able to relinquish the rings. I should have danced a jig at the prospect of a huge pile of money. Instead, I'd felt unexpectedly sentimental. Edward hadn't always been dictatorial. Once, we'd been happy. And my rings had reminded me of that. Adam had been right. I wasn't ready to let go of them, or those memories, quite yet.

The man slumbering beside me was, of course, another unexpected complication, but he was also a pleasant surprise. If I was honest with myself, I found Adam very attractive. I always had. And, of course, I'd always known he was easy to be with. And—

Stop! I admonished myself. That way was madness. The last thing I needed was to jump into anything as ill-conceived as an attraction to a former friend. No, the only man I was going to moon around after was the mysterious Jack Smith. He was the only one who had the power to give me back everything I had lost. He was the only man I could think about right now.

By the time I'd skimmed Austen's letters yet again, the train was approaching the station at Bath Spa, and I nudged Adam awake. "We're here."

"*Hmm?*" He roused and opened one eye. "What?"

"We're in Bath."

He sat up, blinking heavily. "Already?"

I laughed. "It's been an hour and a half."

"I don't believe you." But he grinned, slow and lazy, and my toes curled. With a deep breath and more resolution than I knew I had, I made them uncurl.

"Come on. Let's go," I said.

"Yes, ma'am."

We made our way off the train and through the high Victorian architecture of the station before emerging into Bath itself. From my research, I knew that the town hadn't changed all that much since Jane Austen's day, although what she would have made of the shops selling tea towels and coffee mugs with her purported silhouette on them, I could only guess. The buildings glowed golden in the sunlight, their classical Georgian lines as elegant and timeless as an Austen novel itself. They were constructed of local limestone and had a honey hue and simplicity that bespoke elegance and good taste, even when the ground floor boasted a takeaway fish-and-chip shop.

"Where are you planning to start?" Adam asked.

I knew, of course, exactly where I was going from studying Google Maps. Through the middle of town, skirting the cathedral and the Roman baths, over Pulteney Bridge and to the outskirts of Sydney Gardens. Miss Golightly could be found in a house on Sydney Place, across from the former pleasure garden. But somehow, between here and there, I had to get rid of Adam, who seemed suddenly nervous. He kept glancing around, as if waiting for brigands to appear and rob him at gunpoint.

"Look," I said, pointing. "I think the parade grounds are that way." The parade grounds were a small park that skirted the main part of the town. "Let's head there."

"I don't understand why she hated this place so much," Adam said, still looking about as we made our way along the street. "It's amazing."

Steep hills rose on either side of the valley. To our right, I could see through the trees to the tops of the buildings of the local university high on the hill. To the left lay the older part of Bath, built in the 1700s, when the town had been a glamorous health retreat. Aristocrats and gentry had come to take the waters—both internally and externally—that flowed from the hot springs beneath the city. And there, ahead of us, the spire of Bath Abbey rose to angelic heights.

"She was a country girl at heart," I said. "Bath would have been alien to everything she'd ever known." I thought of our visit to Steventon only a few days before. The bustling spa town would have been the antithesis of Austen's backwater country village. "No wonder she fainted when her parents told her they were moving."

Jane Austen had been twenty-five when her father retired, in modern parlance, and her parents decided to sell off all the furniture and books and everything she had held dear to move to lodgings in Bath. Now I wondered if somehow her relationship with Jack Smith had played a part in forming her dislike for the town. Had she wanted to remain in Hampshire merely because it was dear and familiar? Or would she have been more likely to see Jack there?

"She was that attached to Hampshire?" Adam asked, echoing my own thoughts.

"I think that's why they didn't tell her until it was a fait accompli," I said. "They never gave her a chance to object."

We stopped alongside a wide stone railing that overlooked the river where it spilled from a causeway just below Pulteney Bridge. The bridge was rather unusual in that it also housed a number of shops along each side, so that it was more like a long building that just happened to straddle the Avon.

"Why don't we meet back here in an hour or two?" I said with a false smile plastered on my face. If I brightened any more, I could replace a standard one-hundred-watt bulb. "I appreciate you coming with me, but I need a little time to just be here in Bath. Just to soak it all in. You know what I mean?"

I could tell from his expression that he didn't have a clue what I was talking about.

"Is this part of what you're not telling me?" he asked, confused.

"Yes, okay? It is. But it's a secret, so I need to go by myself."

"Go? I thought you just needed to *be*." The teasing light in his eyes made my stomach twist in a not necessarily unpleasant way.

"Adam . . ."

"All right, all right." He looked at his watch. "Can we meet for a late lunch? I don't like eating by myself."

"Why don't we meet at Sally Lunn's at one o'clock," I said, pleased with my suggestion. The little tea shop had been famous for its eponymous buns since well before Jane Austen's time.

"Isn't that a little touristy?"

I looked around at the open-air double-decker buses touting their services and the Jane Austen memorabilia that occupied almost every shop window. "Is there something here that isn't?"

Adam nodded. "Actually, there's quite a bit. Which you ought to know, if you're the Austen scholar you claim to be."

"*Humph.*" I didn't have a good reply for that, because he was right, so I settled for looking indignant.

"Fine. We'll meet at Sally Lunn's at one." He paused. "Just be careful, Emma. Please."

"Careful? Of what? I'm doing research, not undercover operations for the CIA." I was half annoyed at his patronizing tone and half thrilled that he cared about my well-being.

"Suit yourself." He shrugged, but I could see that I'd annoyed him.

"I appreciate your concern." I knew better than to reach over and put my hand on his arm. I didn't need any reminders of the strength I would feel there. "Please understand. I just need to do this on my own."

"Okay." His expression relaxed. "I'll see you later."

With that, he turned and made his way toward the Abbey and the Roman baths, eating up the pavement with purposeful strides. If I hadn't known better, I would have thought that he had an appointment of his own to keep. And I was left there, beside the parade grounds that flanked the River Avon, to consider whether keeping a secret was worth alienating the one ally I had left.

⚜⚜⚜⚜⚜

The interior of Miss Hester Golightly's home on Sydney Place did not look quite as I had pictured it. In my imagination, I had seen Axminster carpets, Staffordshire china dogs, perhaps a Robert Adam mantelpiece—all straight out of an Austen novel and one-hundred-percent English. Instead, when the diminutive woman, a dead ringer for Judi Dench, waved me inside, I found myself in a monochromatic homage to contemporary interior design. The outside of the building might have been purely Georgian, but inside, all was sleek and modern.

"Miss Grant, how lovely that you could visit," Miss Golightly said as she led me into the lounge. The sofa was so pristine that it hurt my eyes to look at it. "Won't you sit down? Would you like some tea?"

I nodded, struck mute. Hester Golightly had frosty blonde hair cut in a pixie style, and she wore trendy jeans with a neon-print hoodie. She indicated that I should take a seat on the sofa. I did so with fear and trembling. I could only hope I hadn't picked up anything on the train that would transfer onto this paean to spotlessness.

"How was your journey?" She lifted the teapot and prepared to pour. "And, please, call me Hester."

"Yes. Fine. Of course." I wasn't prepared for this . . . normalness, if that was even a word. I carefully sat down on the sofa.

Hester laughed. "You're gobsmacked!" She reached over from her perch on a chair next to me and patted my knee. "They always are, poor dears, when they come here after spending time with Mrs. Parrot. We couldn't be more different, could we?"

I decided that was a rhetorical question. Miss Golightly hardly paused for breath before she continued. "Well, you've made it this far, so that's a good sign. Mrs. Parrot never sends me anyone she's not absolutely certain of." She started to hand me the cup and saucer and then drew it back. "I forgot to ask. Milk? Sugar?"

"No, thank you." I reached for the china cup, in need of the unadulterated caffeine.

"So, you've come here and are no doubt full of questions." She smiled mysteriously. "That's the best part, you know, of being a Formidable. So many delicious, juicy questions."

I took a sip of the tea, which scalded my tongue. Tears of pain stung my eyes, but I persevered. "My understanding is that I have to complete a task that you give me."

She leaned back in her chair and sipped her own tea without flinching at its heat. "Of course. That too. It wouldn't be nearly as much fun without them."

As much fun for whom? I wanted to ask, but I didn't. "Mrs. Parrot seemed to discourage questions, or else answer them cryptically."

"Yes, well, she rather enjoys her role as the gatekeeper. Sometimes she enjoys it a bit too much, the rest of us think."

The rest of us? Just how many of them were there? Before I could ask, she continued. "So, I take it you've put the pieces together about Jack Smith."

"I think so." My tea had cooled enough so that I could take a careful sip. I was so afraid of spilling a drop on that sofa, my hand trembled. "He was a student of her father's, and they must have developed a fondness for one another at Steventon. At least there was a fondness on her part, given what she wrote in the parish register."

"Yes. Very good. Then you're ready for the next step."

"What's that?"

Hester set her cup on the table. "What did Jane Austen love more than anything?" she asked with a smile.

I paused, searching for the right answer. She had loved her family, reading, visiting friends. And writing novels, obviously. But she had adored one thing above all else.

"Dancing," I replied. "She loved dancing." Her published letters, as well as those of family and friends, all corroborated the belief that Austen had been an inveterate dancer.

"She may have disliked Bath," Hester said, "but she loved the balls at the Assembly Rooms." With a flourish, she reached for an envelope that sat next to her teacup. "You may read this now."

"Before I complete the task?"

"Yes."

With eager hands, I took the envelope from her and ripped it open with all the eagerness of a kid attacking a pile of presents under the Christmas tree.

"Careful, there," Hester warned me. "That's the original."

My hands stilled instantly. "The original?"

"I thought you might be weary of copies."

"*Um*, yes. I mean, are you sure?" I looked up at her, and she was smiling at my confusion.

"Mrs. Parrot tends to fuss over the letters as if they're holy writ, but I find it far better to allow my visitors to handle them." She shot me a warning look. "Very carefully, of course."

"Yes. Certainly." Now I was as cautious as I had been impatient only a few moments before.

I thought of the letter I'd seen in the British Library— encased behind glass, exposed only to the dim lighting of the gallery. Perhaps Hester Golightly was being a bit reckless with such a treasure, but that didn't stop me from reaching inside the envelope and drawing out the yellowed piece of paper there.

The familiar, even handwriting made my heart beat more quickly. My breath caught when I saw the inscription at the top.

BATH, 3 JUNE 1801

And then the greeting.

My dearest Jack . . .

My first thought was that it was a forgery. The paper fluttered in my shaking hands. "She can't have written to him," I said to Hester, who was watching me with a bemused expression. "Not unless—" I fell silent at the implication of the piece of paper in my hand.

"Not unless she was engaged to him," Hester finished for me. "The plot thickens, as they say."

I looked again at the date on the letter. It had been written from Bath shortly after her family moved there in May 1801. I knew, without having to consult any of my research books, that no Austen letters survived from the period between that move in May and the autumn of 1804, a lengthy gap that had never been adequately explained.

Most scholars attributed her silence to Austen's dislike of Bath. But it had never made sense to me that an avid correspondent like Jane Austen would simply abandon the practice because she was unhappy with her living situation. In fact, the opposite seemed more likely to me—that she would have

written a greater number of letters in her attempts to stay con-
nected to Steventon and her Hampshire friends.

> *. . . when I see you again at the ball on Wednesday.*
> *My new dress displeases Cassandra, but I like it above*
> *all things and shall consider myself in the first stare of*
> *fashion . . .*

"But if she wrote to him, surely they would have been
engaged?"

If nothing else, Jane Austen had been rather a stickler for
propriety, as an impoverished gentleman's daughter had to
be to safeguard the only thing of value she possessed—her
reputation. I thought of Marianne in *Sense and Sensibility* and
the flurry of letters she sent to the duplicitous Willoughby.
Marianne's mother and sister had taken the letters as tacit
proof of an engagement. But they had been mistaken. Was I
mistaken, too, to assume that Austen would only correspond
with a gentleman if she were betrothed to him?

"One would think so," Hester Golightly said with a lift of
her eyebrows. "Yet that letter contains no undying declarations
of love. Perhaps she was a bit more scandalous than we have
been led to believe."

I did some quick mental math. Jane Austen would have
been twenty-six or so when she wrote the letter. From the contents, I surmised that Jack Smith was expected to come to Bath

shortly after she and her parents arrived. They were to dance at the Assembly Rooms. And then what had happened? I turned the letter over to see the address where she had sent it.

Sidmouth. A resort town Austen and her family had visited in the summer of 1801. Had they gone there purposely so that she could see her fiancé? Lieutenant Jack Smith would have wanted to stay near the coast so that he could appear quickly when ordered to duty on his ship.

"There's no way a generally known engagement could have been kept quiet," I said, half to Hester Golightly and half to myself. "Cassandra might have excised and hidden away her sister's letters, but she didn't have the ability to censor everyone else's correspondence."

"So it must have been a secret engagement, then," Hester said with a smile. "Or a shocking impropriety."

"I wouldn't have expected it of her."

"Perhaps it is in the unexpected that we are truly known." Hester made the pronouncement as if she were the oracle at Delphi.

"I'm so confused." I carefully refolded the letter and slid it back into the envelope. "I don't know what to believe anymore."

"Have some more tea, dear," Hester said, reaching for the pot and refilling my cup. "I always find that helps."

"So what's my task, then?" I asked before she had finished pouring. I couldn't imagine what they would pair with that letter that would match it for import and surprise.

Hester looked up. "Why, you must dance at the Assembly Rooms, of course."

Dance? At the Assembly Rooms? I laughed. "You're joking."

She set the teapot back on the tray. "Oh no, dear. I would never joke about dancing."

"And who am I supposed to dance with?" I could picture myself now, twirling in the middle of a gaggle of tourists.

"You must dance with a handsome young man, just as Jane would have done. Then will you have an inkling as to how she felt when she was here in Bath."

"Miss Golightly—"

"Hester, dear. And really, this task isn't all that difficult. Do you know any men in Bath?"

I thought of Adam, wandering around and waiting to meet me at Sally Lunn's. "The one I came here with," I said with great reluctance.

"That's perfect, then." Hester clasped her hands together in delight. "I could drum one up for you, of course, but it's much better if it's someone you know. Someone you're attracted to."

"I'm not attracted to—"

"But of course you must be." She waved a dismissive hand. "You brought him to Bath. Now finish your tea, dear. The Assembly Rooms await."

"What do I do afterward?"

"Afterward?"

"Yes. Do I come here? Will you give me another letter?"

"Oh, dear me. I suppose you go back to London and see Mrs. Parrot again."

"You don't seem very sure."

"Well, to tell the truth, dear, this is the point where most of our . . . inquirers decide that we're a bunch of batty old geezers and tell us to go stuff ourselves." She laughed. "You're a refreshing change of pace."

Great. So I was not among the sensible majority. "Miss Golightly—"

"Hester, dear. Now run along with you." She stood up, and I automatically did the same. "You'll want some lunch before you make the trek up the hill to the Assembly Rooms."

I didn't even know if they were open. I certainly didn't know if Mrs. Parrot and Hester Golightly were part of some sort of bizarre Austenian conspiracy. And I definitely didn't know how I was going to persuade Adam to dance with me, but the sight of that envelope, still lying on the table beside the tea tray, galvanized me.

Besides, I really had no other choice. I'd put all my eggs in the one basket. I was out of options.

"So nice to meet you, dear," Hester said as she escorted me to the door. "I hope you and your young man have a lovely day in Bath."

"Thank you." I didn't know what else to say.

"No need." She reached out and gave me a quick hug. "I'm

sure you'll do very well. Just follow your heart. I've always found that to be the very thing for getting what I wanted."

I didn't want to argue with her, to tell her that so far in my life, following my heart had led me down the road to disaster, so I simply nodded, said my good-byes, and turned toward the center of town.

bviously there was only one thing to do. I had to meet Jack . . . I mean, Adam. I had to meet Adam and drag him to the Assembly Rooms and persuade him to dance with me. But first I would butter him up with lunch.

Sally Lunn's house on Parade Passage was the oldest in Bath, a remnant from pre-Georgian times. Local legend had it that the young French woman appeared in the town in the late 1600s and began selling her eponymous buns. The restaurant still served the famous bread, along with all manner of sweet and savory toppings. I'd read about Sally Lunn buns but never tried them.

I arrived at the restaurant at the appointed meeting time, but there was no sign of Adam. I was afraid to go looking for him, afraid he would turn up if I wandered away, so I stood by the front window of the restaurant, shifting from one foot to the other, trying not to look as if I was being stood up.

Five minutes passed. Then ten. And after half an hour, I
knew that Adam wasn't coming. My heart sank lower, inch by
inch, until it rested somewhere around the soles of my shoes.
Adam seemed so trustworthy, and he'd been so keen to help
me. Had he hopped a train back to London? Found a better
lunch date there in Bath? I had no idea, and no way to get in
touch with him.

With a sigh of resignation, I turned away from Sally Lunn's
and struck out toward the abbey. I would skirt it and then find
one of the long streets that would take me up the steep hill to
the Upper Assembly Rooms. Even if I couldn't find a dancing
partner, I still wanted to see the place and at least imagine what
Jane Austen must have felt when she danced there.

The climb to the top of the hill was not an inconsiderable
one, and long before I reached the top, I was huffing and puffing. No wonder genteel women in Austen's day had waited for
a sedan chair so that a couple of burly porters could provide
the necessary muscle. At last, though, I found myself in front
of the Assembly Rooms. The main entrance looked like a small
Greek temple with its triangular pediment and supporting col-
umns. I stepped underneath and let myself inside.

The Assembly Rooms had been the site of balls, concerts,
card parties, and other entertainments in Jane Austen's day. It
consisted of four major areas—the Octagon, which functioned
as a sort of central hallway, the Card Room, the Tea Room,
and, finally, the Ball Room. I had read about them, of course,
but like so much on my journey thus far, I wasn't prepared for

their splendor, or for how little they had changed since Austen's day.

"May I help you?"

I turned to my right to see a woman of about fifty approaching me. Her slim skirt and no-nonsense hairdo spoke volumes.

"Yes. I wanted to look around if I could."

She frowned, shook her head. "I'm sorry, but we're closed at the moment."

Closed? "I'm sorry, the sign on the door said—"

"We're closed for a private party this evening."

I looked around. Other than this woman and myself, there wasn't a soul in the place. She must have read my thoughts from my expression.

"The florists will be here any minute. We have a private reception for a corporate client."

"Please, could I look around very quickly? I've come all the way from the States just to see these rooms." Well, I had, in a sense. I wasn't fudging the truth that much.

"Miss—"

"Professor," I said, unashamedly. "Professor Grant." I even dropped the name of my former school.

The woman's whole demeanor changed. "Are you doing research?"

I made myself relax and smile. "Jane Austen."

The woman nodded sagely. "Of course. Well," she said as she looked down at her watch, "I suppose it wouldn't hurt for you to look around for a few minutes."

"Thank you." I moved toward the nearest open door and stepped inside.

One by one, I immersed myself in the glory of the assembly rooms. Their simplicity made them beautiful, and every surface that could be polished had been buffed until it shone. The gilt, the high ceilings, the intricate detail of the adornments —I was high as a kite by the time I entered the expanse of the ballroom.

Step by careful step, I moved to the center of the space. Icy blue walls with gleaming white carved moldings surrounded me, and the vast expanse of the shining hardwood floor spread in every direction. It was glorious. It was awe-inspiring. And it was very, very empty.

I looked over my shoulder toward the entrance to make sure I was alone. And then, feeling completely foolish, I began to hum a tune under my breath. I'd seen the dances of Jane Austen's day performed in movies, and even at the occasional academic conference where a dance instructor had been brought in to lighten the atmosphere.

I moved forward, then back, trying the best I could to mimic the dipping sways and turns. I imagined that I was Jane Austen, unhappy about my family's removal to Bath but eager to see Jack Smith again. He was in town, he had promised to be at the ball. Uncertainty. Excitement. I tried to feel them, tried to channel her churning emotions across the course of two hundred years.

I was utterly, completely unable to do so.

"What are you doing?"

My head snapped up and I whirled around. Adam stood in the doorway, watching me with a look of amusement.

"I'm dancing. What does it look like?" Anger shot through my midsection, sharp and surprising. "Not that it's any of your business."

He stepped forward, his head bowed just enough to suggest penance. "I'm sorry, Em. I lost track of the time. If I hadn't seen you headed up Milsom Street—"

I waved a hand in dismissal. "Whatever. It was just lunch." I hardened my heart, because I had to. In the course of a few days, Adam had lured me into letting my guard down. After all I'd been through with Edward, I should have known better. Men were men. But mostly, they were dogs.

"If you had a cell phone—"

"Well, I don't." I didn't mean to snap quite so harshly. "Look, like I said, it's no big deal."

Adam moved forward again, and I felt rather like an antelope being stalked by a lion.

"Looks like you need a partner." He grinned, a decidedly lopsided and thoroughly charming expression. No wonder he'd been able to get me those books at the British Library so quickly. No woman could resist that kind of masculine appeal.

"Here. Allow me." He reached out and took my hand in his, then settled his other hand at my waist.

"What are you doing?"

"I'm trying to waltz with you."

"Jane Austen didn't waltz. That didn't come along until later. It was all minuets and gavottes and country dances."

"Then what do you want me to do?"

I had no idea how to minuet or gavotte or even manage a country dance. My shoulder sagged in defeat. "All right, then. We'll waltz." Maybe it would be close enough for whatever purpose the Formidables expected it to serve.

My objection to the waltz wasn't on the grounds of historical accuracy, actually. The truth was that I didn't want to be so close to Adam. A moment later, though, I had no choice in the matter, and somehow, my free hand found my way to his shoulder.

"What should we do for music?" he asked.

I wanted to die of mortification on the spot. I was far too old, too jaded, and too hurt to be caught up in the romance of such a moment, but apparently Edward's humiliation wasn't sufficient to inoculate me against the combined power of a ballroom, a Jane Austen fantasy, and Adam.

"We could hum," I said, and I hated the flush that rose in my cheeks.

And then, from nowhere, I heard music. Real music. A piano, and it was playing a waltz. The soft strains drifted in from the open doorway. Someone was playing the instrument in the Octagon just outside, probably practicing for the reception that evening.

I looked up to see Adam staring at me with a very odd look on his face. "Does this happen to you a lot?" he asked.

"Does what happen to me?"

"You know. Weird coincidences. Whatever you need appearing in the nick of time."

"I would hardly say that whatever I need shows up in any time, nick or not."

Adam shook his head. "My being at Anne-Elise's house. Your free pass to the British Library. And now ghostly music." He looked me over with caution. "If I didn't know better, I would say that you're following some sort of script. Or at least your life is."

I stopped to consider his words. "You know," I said, realizing for the first time how strange it was, indeed, that I should be in this time, in this place, with this man, "you may be right."

And with that, he moved into the steps of the dance, and we were whirling our way across the vast expanse of the floor. The polished hardwood beneath my feet was like glass, and even in my Pumas, I glided like an angel. Adam had obviously had a few lessons somewhere along the line. He would have done any Jane Austen hero proud.

Before too long I was out of breath, but I didn't want to stop. The enormous crystal chandeliers above me sparkled with light, and the pale blue walls of the room with their white molding made it seem as if we were dancing among the clouds. Adam's hand was firmly holding my waist, his other balancing me as we spun around and around. No wonder Jane Austen had loved it so much. No wonder she—

I stumbled, my feet tangling with Adam's, and for a moment I thought we might both collapse in an ignominious heap on the floor. Then he righted himself, and me with him, and we were safe. Only we were no longer spinning and whirling. We weren't even touching. Instead, we were standing in the middle of the ballroom, breathing heavily and looking at each other with a new kind of wariness.

Imagine to yourself everything most profligate and shocking in the way of dancing . . .

Austen's words from her earliest letter, at least her earliest known until now, haunted me. She'd been describing another suitor named Tom Lefroy, not Jack Smith, but her words might have been born earlier, with Jack. In a moment like this.

"It's time to go," I said, not even pretending to look at my watch. "We don't want to miss our train."

Adam frowned. "Emma—"

"Besides, I was only supposed to be in here for a minute. Technically, they're closed. I don't know how you got in here anyway."

"I charmed the dragon guarding the gate. Em—" He reached out, and I stepped away.

"We'd better—" But I wasn't quick enough. He caught me by the elbow. His grip was firm but not painful.

"Emma, please don't—"

"Look." I pointed toward the doorway, where the dragon lady stood with her arms crossed and her lips pursed into a thin line. "I think we're in trouble."

I started toward the door. Behind me, I heard Adam respond.

"Think? You *think* we're in trouble?"

For the sake of self-preservation, I pretended I hadn't heard him. I kept moving, fleeing, all in the guise of polite behavior.

The woman gave me a cold nod as I approached. "I really must ask you to leave now," she said.

"Of course. We were just on our way out."

I could hear Adam's footsteps. He would catch up with me in a few moments, but I still had precious seconds to school my expression to careful neutrality.

"Thank you," I heard him say to the woman, and then he was beside me as we made our way through the Octagon and out the front door.

Dark clouds had gathered, and thunder rumbled ominously in the distance. I looked up, prepared to find that the heavens were about to unleash their fury, but small pockets of sunlight still shined through.

"You can't run forever, Em" was all Adam said as we started off down the steep hill again toward the center of town and the train station.

I didn't answer. What could I say? Now the only friendship I still had, however unexpected, had been upended. I was tired of being adrift. Tired of romance and attraction and all the complications and ruination it entailed. Tired of trying to find some pattern, divine or not, in what had happened, what was happening to me. Most of all, though, I was tired of Jane Austen ruining my life.

As we half slid down the steep pavement that led to the

center of town, I renewed my vow to even the score with her. Her promise of a happy ending had led me into torment and trouble. Could I truly be blamed if I exposed her for the fraud she was? Surely I would be doing women everywhere a good turn.

As I walked along beside Adam, though, and the rain began to fall, I knew that my rationalizations were just that. Weak attempts to justify my own need to pack my heart, and my feelings, away forever. Because I knew, as sure as anything, that I would never again be able to withstand the kind of betrayal Edward had perpetrated on me, and I wasn't nearly as strong as I would have liked to believe.

I did not come to England to fall in love.
I did not come to England to fall in love.

f I had been my third-grade teacher, I would have made myself write that sentence one hundred times on the blackboard. Clearly, my third-grade teacher was rather old school, but then again, everyone knows that repetition is the key to learning.

Adam and I had returned to London from Bath the day before in relative silence. Other than a few words of stilted, polite conversation, we'd kept to ourselves, reading on the train home and parting company once we reached Anne-Elise's town house. I climbed the stairs to my bedroom, suddenly exhausted, although the day had been taxing more from a mental standpoint than a physical one.

Adam went straight to the computer in the sitting room, and he was still there later that night when I crept downstairs to get a glass of water. I wondered what he was up to but didn't want to ask, because asking would have entailed conversation, which I was working hard to avoid.

I should never have danced with him. For that matter, I shouldn't have allowed him to accompany me to Bath. But despite my resolution to be done with men, I couldn't will away the palpable sense of loneliness. I might have given up on happy endings, but being resigned to my solitary fate didn't do away with the need for companionship.

I set out extra early the next morning for South Kensington so that I could continue avoiding Adam. I was too afraid even to make coffee in the kitchen. I waited patiently outside the Starbucks on the High Street until a bleary-eyed barista finally took pity on me and let me in. Then, armed with a venti latte for extra oomph, I made my way to Mrs. Parrot's doorstep.

This time, Mrs. Parrot hadn't wanted to chat. I didn't know whether it was the hour or whether she had some secret meeting of the Formidables going on in the lounge, but whatever the case, she was all business. She didn't even quiz me about whether I'd completed my task in the Assembly Rooms. Honestly, she looked rather harried—orange hair uncombed, flecks of lipstick on her teeth—and she kept me standing on the front steps while she retrieved two envelopes from a table just inside the door. She pressed them into my hands hastily.

BETH PATTILLO ❧ *150*
BETH PATTILLO ❧ *150*

"Come back when you're done," she said before shooing me down the steps and shutting the door to number 22 firmly behind her.

The envelope on top was marked *Open First*, so I did. I expected a note or some other sort of instructions. Instead, I found two theater tickets for a performance of Sheridan's *The Rivals* that evening at a theater near Covent Garden.

"I guess I'm going to the theater," I mumbled to myself. An elegant lady walking a large standard poodle gave me a curious look as she passed by me. *Great.* Now I was making a habit of talking to myself in public.

The second envelope was marked *Open Afterward*. I presumed that meant after the play. With a sigh, I tucked the tickets back into the first envelope, stuck both envelopes into my purse, and headed off in the direction of the Underground station. Now I just had to figure out something to do for the rest of the day, because the last thing in the world I wanted to do was go back to Hampstead and Adam.

❧❧❧❧

When I arrived at Covent Garden, the stores weren't even open. Once upon a time, the area had been home to a thriving produce and flower market, but today it held upscale shops and boutiques, along with restaurants that ran the gamut from trendy chains to some of London's oldest dining establishments.

Now, though, in the hazy morning light, the cobbled streets

were sparsely filled with shopgirls on their way to work and the occasional delivery man on his morning rounds. Luckily, I found a branch of Boots, the popular drugstore, open for business. I ducked inside and emerged a few minutes later with an unexpected purchase—a notebook and pen. I stuffed these in my purse next to the envelopes Mrs. Parrot had given me and resumed my meanderings.

The center of Covent Garden boasts an early Victorian arcade whose light-filled, vaulted canopy feels like a smaller version of the great train stations of London. I walked the length of the enclosure, watching as the open-air vendors set up their wares for the day. Edward would have rolled his eyes at their kitschy, secondhand goods, but I found its shabby genteel air rather charming.

At the other end of the arcade, I emerged to find myself looking at St. Paul's Church—not the famous cathedral but the smaller one built for the Duke of Bedford and later made famous in the opening scene of *My Fair Lady*. It was another sight I would never have seen had I been with Edward. He would have deplored the whole area as a tourist mecca, but I was charmed.

In Austen's day, Covent Garden was still a produce market. I could imagine her here, while she was staying with her brother Henry in nearby Henrietta Street. Perhaps she had helped to shop for the day's supply of potatoes and peas. Perhaps she had arranged to meet Jack Smith while she was shopping, quite by accident, of course.

These thoughts entertained me as I completed my circum-navigation of the market. By then, I was starving, and I was more than ready to find a small café and order coffee and a croissant. First, though, I wanted to wander around to Henrietta Street and see where Jane had stayed, however briefly, when she'd been in London.

A few minutes' walk brought me to my destination. The row of Georgian terraced houses was taller and more severe than my current roost in Hampstead, but the classical simplicity remained the same. I spotted the green plaque that marked where Austen had stayed—not one of the famous blue plaques, for she had not actually lived there. Still, I remembered reading that this marker, put up by the City of Westminster, was the only tribute to an Austen residence in London.

I loitered on the opposite sidewalk, noting the dates on the plaque. She had stayed there between 1813 and 1815, long after her early infatuation with Jack Smith, so perhaps there were no meetings in Covent Garden as I'd imagined. But had he still been a part of her life then? She would have been in her late thirties, at least.

There were many questions still unanswered, and I had no idea how long Mrs. Parrot intended to drag this out. Shaking my head, I turned to head down the street . . .

And ran smack into Barry.

"Emma!" He grabbed my shoulders to steady me. I looked up and was immediately weak-kneed at the sight of his sexy grin. "Did I hurt you?"

"No, no. I'm fine." I stepped back, and his hands fell away. "What are you doing here?" I had thought he would have left for Italy by now.

"I could ask you the same thing." He looked around. "What's the attraction?" His eyes landed on the green plaque on the building opposite where we stood. "Hot on the Austen trail, huh?"

I shook my head. "At this point, I don't know what I am." I still couldn't believe the coincidence, running into him again. "So, am I stalking you, or are you stalking me?"

He shrugged and smiled. "I don't care, as long as it ends up with us together." He glanced at his watch. "Let me buy you some breakfast."

I knew I was playing with fire. A gorgeous bad boy combined with my need to run away from my fledgling feelings for Adam—even I could see that I was assembling the ingredients of a recipe for disaster.

I hesitated but Barry didn't. "You don't have to be anywhere, do you?" he said. "Everybody has time for breakfast."

"I guess." It was not exactly my most gracious acceptance, but I was locked in a death battle with my better judgment.

"How about that French café around the corner?"

I nodded, not entirely certain which restaurant he meant, but the choice of café wasn't what I was worried about.

"What are you doing out and about so early?" I asked him, ready to deflect the conversation away from myself.

"Sophie had another spa day booked around here, and she's still not comfortable on the Underground by herself."

"Oh." What else could I offer as a reply? Despite being born and bred a good Southern girl, I'd never been able to pull off the helpless female routine with any success. The Sophies of the world possessed a secret knowledge I hadn't been given.

"Here it is." Barry pointed to the black storefront with *Paul* stenciled in gold letters. The rest of the sign advertised the place as a boulangerie and patisserie.

Barry led the way inside, past the black-and-white-tiled floor of the takeaway area in front and into the back room, with intimate tables and gaily colored murals on the walls.

"How's this?" he asked, pulling a chair out for me at a table for two in the corner. His action nullified the question.

No modern woman worth her salt would admit it, but sometimes it's a relief when a man takes charge. This truth is only operative, though, when a woman has the means and the power to tell him to cut it out when it gets annoying. I'd learned this basic fact all too well after I'd married Edward and become emotionally and financially dependent on him.

The waitress appeared, deposited our menus while charming Barry and ignoring me, and then disappeared only long enough to return with a pot of coffee. Soon enough, we'd given her our order—crepes for Barry, an omelette for me—and she couldn't find another reason to linger by our table.

"Does Sophie mind that?" I asked, nodding toward the waitress's disappearing back.

Barry shrugged with a self-satisfied expression that was one-hundred-percent male. "I don't know. She's never said anything."

Of course not, I wanted to say, because that's how the game is played when you're trying to catch a man. But I refrained.

"So did you really come to Covent Garden just to see a plaque?" Barry asked.

I shook my head. "No. I wanted to do some shopping, but I was way too early." I wasn't about to admit that I couldn't go home because I was having unwanted feelings for my house-mate. "I thought I'd just wander around, and I wanted to scout out a theater. I've got tickets to a play tonight."

"What are you seeing?"

"Sheridan's *The Rivals*."

Barry nodded in approval. "Good choice. Can't go wrong with eighteenth-century drama."

"You really are an egghead, aren't you?" I said with a teasing smile. "Despite the macho Hemingway thing."

"Don't tell. It would ruin my image." Then he winked at me. "You'll keep my secret, right?"

That wink, that conspiratorial tone, was undermining any higher-minded impulses I could muster. How many women—coeds, grad students, other professors' wives—crumpled like a house of cards under the assault of his charms?

"Who's going with you?" Barry asked.

"Where?" I was still recovering from that wink.

"You mentioned tickets. Plural. Who are you taking?"

"Oh. *Um . . .*" I didn't want to say "No one" because that would have sounded pathetic, but I didn't want to lie either. The only other person in London I knew to invite was Adam, and no way was I going there.

"You, if you're free," I said with a decisiveness that was as forced as it was unusual for me. "Unless you have plans with Sophie—"

Despite Barry's almost compulsive attempts to win me over, what could be safer than a man who already had another woman trying to reel him in?

"What time?" Barry said, looking eager.

I told him the curtain time, and then he leaned back in his chair with a look of masculine satisfaction on his face. "Should I meet you there?"

"Yes. But at the risk of repeating myself, won't Sophie mind?" Even though I had no designs on Barry, my conscience bothered me a little bit.

He waved away my question with a practiced hand. "We're only colleagues. She can manage without me for one night."

His answer sparked a flame of discomfort in the vicinity of my conscience. "She's a very understanding woman."

"Colleague," he corrected me. "We're just colleagues."

And I could see, in that moment, that he truly believed what he was saying. The question was whether the unseen Sophie would agree with his description of their relationship.

"So you're not a couple?" In a way, I was prying, but I was also intrigued by this unfettered access to the male psyche.

He shrugged. "I don't like labels. They're too limiting."

Especially to his libido. "What about Sophie? Isn't she looking for a happily-ever-after?"

Barry laughed. "You're kidding, right?"

I shook my head. "I'm not."

"You've been reading too much Jane Austen," he said, and I couldn't really disagree with that.

"So you don't believe in happy endings?" I asked.

"Is that really what you want from a relationship?" Barry asked, eyebrows arched. "An ending?"

"It's a figure of speech. It's not meant to be literal."

"It is when women use it." Barry crossed his arms over his chest. "Where did women get the idea that once a man commits to marriage, it's all over?" He uncrossed his arms, put them on the table, and leaned toward me. "That's just the beginning."

I frowned. "You don't seem like the kind of guy to have a lot of experience with commitment." And then I was afraid I might have offended him, but he appeared unfazed.

"That's where you're wrong. I've been married. Twice. Never again, though. Wedding vows make women lose their minds. They think the tough part's over."

A flush stung my cheeks, because I was certainly guilty as charged. I had thought that once Edward and I were married, the rest would be smooth sailing. After all, isn't that what Austen had promised in her novels? That if a woman was sensible enough to marry for love, the rest would be a piece of cake?

"I don't think it's fair to generalize about all women," I said in a weak attempt to defend my gender.

"Maybe. Maybe not. But you can't deny that men are much more pragmatic. We don't set ourselves up to be disillusioned."

Was that what I had done when I'd fallen in love with Edward and married him? Was any romantic relationship merely a disaster waiting to happen once the shiny newness wore off?

The waitress reappeared with our food. When Barry barely acknowledged her, she slammed the plates down with a thunk and stomped off.

"Do you want to have dinner before the play?" he asked, but I shook my head.

"I'll just meet you at the theater."

I needed some time to think about what he had said, to sit with his words and sift through them for any nuggets of truth. Had my unrealistic expectations played as much a part in the demise of my marriage as Edward's infidelity? I didn't want to believe it could be true, but the notion had taken hold in my mind, put down roots, and was determined to grow.

"Dinner afterward, then," Barry said. "Have you ever been to the Ivy?"

I had, but did it matter? His suggestion was meant to impress me. If he could score a same-day reservation for a table at one of the most sought-after restaurants in town, I actually would be impressed. Even Edward couldn't have pulled that off.

"Sounds great." I lifted my fork and dug into my omelette. I had a feeling I was going to need my strength, because a day that had started off very strangely now promised to get even more surreal. And I hadn't even opened the second envelope yet.

CHAPTER
FIFTEEN

ith almost the full day
in front of me, I said
good-bye to Barry and
ambled off down Long
Acre toward Charing Cross Road. That busy thoroughfare had
long been synonymous with bookstores, and what better way
to kill a day than by immersing myself in them?

By the third shop, though, I was overwhelmed and irrita-
ble. I kept walking in the direction of the Thames and found
myself in once-familiar territory. Just before Trafalgar Square,
there on my right, was one of my favorite places in London.
The National Portrait Gallery.

Most people, of course, preferred the centuries of
European masterpieces at the larger National Gallery that
fronted Trafalgar Square. But the Regency rooms at the
Portrait Gallery, not to mention the restaurant on the top floor,

whose windows presented diners with a Peter Pan-like view of London's skyline, were something of a spiritual home for me. Any Austen aficionado, much less a true devotee, could revel for an entire afternoon in the Gainsborough and Reynolds portraits of luminaries like Admiral Nelson, Lord Byron, and King George III.

I ducked through the glass doors and made my way up the steps, then up the escalator to the third floor. My indulgence at this particular museum had been one of which Edward approved, although I'd had to feign interest as we wandered through all the other rooms before I finally lured him to the Regency Galleries.

While I loved the elegant portraits by the most renowned artists of that day, my favorite portrait had little, if any, artistic merit. It was also quite small, no more than a few inches square. The subject's sister had done a quick study in pencil and water-color, left half finished, and no relative of the subject had ever thought it much resembled the person who posed for it.

Still, it was the only authenticated portrait of Jane Austen known to exist.

In the room dedicated to the artists and writers of the early nineteenth century, I paused before a small wooden pillar, not more than three feet high, topped with a glass case. As I stepped toward it, a dim light within the case flickered on, casting a pale glow over the picture.

There she was. She stared back at me, half slumped in a

chair with her arms crossed over her chest. A cap of some kind covered her head, with a few dark, curly tendrils escaping to dance across her forehead. She looked a little annoyed but not unpleasant, as if someone had interrupted her work, but since she loved that someone, she would tolerate the interruption. Her eyes were dark, her face round, her nose strong. I had seen portraits of her father, and I thought she resembled him. No known portrait of her mother existed. In fact, of all eight Austen children, only two never sat for a formal portrait—Jane and her brother George, who had been mentally handicapped or epileptic or somehow physically challenged. George had been farmed out to caretakers in a nearby village at an early age, so his lack of a portrait wasn't surprising. But Jane? Surely her family had suggested one.

I believed, judging from her expression in this authenticated picture, that she'd hated having her image taken with as much ferocity as she adored painting verbal pictures of her characters.

I stepped back, and the light flicked off, leaving Austen in the dark once more. I stepped forward. Illumination. Back. Shrouded in mystery once more. The symbolism wasn't exactly subtle.

Around me, visitors moved through the galleries, and when one or two stopped to see the Austen portrait, I graciously stepped aside. I stayed there, though, for a long while, studying her in both the light and the dark. She seemed so small when compared with the other great figures of her day, whose images were captured on enormous canvases that dominated the high-ceilinged rooms around me.

Austen had been unknown to the public in her lifetime. Her books had been published with the simple attribution *By A Lady* or *By the Author of*, although her fans included the Prince Regent, later to become King George IV. Because she was a gentleman's daughter, the stench of trade prevented her from exposing herself publicly. But here she was in spite of that, in this room. The most modest, and yet in the minds of many, the greatest English novelist of them all.

Austen could so easily have been lost to history, had her father not championed her writing, had her brother Henry not been willing to act as her agent, had her family and friends not enjoyed her work and complimented her on her abilities and encouraged her to continue writing. The very existence of her novels was a miracle.

That thought, that moment, standing in front of her portrait, renewed in me a desire I hadn't experienced in years. I slipped my purse off my shoulder and dug around in it, fumbling for the notebook and pen I'd purchased that morning. I looked around, eager for a place to sit, but this particular gallery didn't have any benches, so I slid to the floor, letting go of any sense of dignity and decorum. Then I uncapped the pen and let it fly across the page.

I didn't know where the words came from, but they'd been

stored up for so long that there were oceans of them, pouring onto the page as quickly as my pen would allow. I must have sat there an hour or more, jotting down random thoughts and semicoherent memories, before a pair of navy slacks appeared beside me. I stopped writing and looked up, up, up to find a frowning security guard staring down from a great height. Well, probably not that great a height, but I was sitting on the floor, after all.

"Miss?" he asked, all British dignity. "Are you ill?"

Which was a polite way, of course, of saying that crazy Americans should get up off the floor and find a proper bench to sit on.

"Um, yeah. I mean, no. No, I'm fine."

With great reluctance, and a few imprecations muttered under my breath, I closed my notebook, put the cap back on my pen, and shoved both into my purse. Getting up off the floor took a minute, but I finally managed it. My legs were numb from sitting in such an unfamiliar position.

"Perhaps you would prefer a bench? There are some in the next room." Again, his tone was polite, but his meaning was clear.

"No, thank you. I believe I'm done in this gallery." I tried to smile brightly, to convince him I wasn't completely off the beam.

"Perhaps a cup of tea . . ." He let the suggestion trail off. "There's a café downstairs, near the bookshop."

"Yes, that sounds lovely. I'll just . . ." I turned and walked away with as much dignity as I could muster.

I didn't actually go to the café, though. Instead, I made my way out of the museum and around the corner to Trafalgar Square. Throngs of people filled the plaza, lunchtime hordes eating their meals on the vast steps or at the feet of the enormous lions that flanked Nelson's Column. Pigeons flew overhead, and traffic whizzed toward the Admiralty Arch and the long promenade of the Mall that led to Buckingham Palace.

Tea was an excellent suggestion. I couldn't fault the security guard for that. Perhaps a sandwich too. I headed off across the square and toward the arch. Just beyond, along the south side of the Mall, lay St. James's Park, yet another oasis of peaceful greenery in the midst of the city. It also boasted an excellent café. It was time to part with more of my precious pound notes, because what had just happened deserved a celebration. I had given in to that deep-seated, almost primeval impulse I'd ignored for years. I'd allowed myself to write. Not academic papers or abstracts or book reviews but real, original, personal writing. It felt glorious.

❧❧❧❧❧

My lunch consisted of a chicken-and-bacon sandwich along with the prescribed cup of tea. I settled onto a bench under a sheltering tree beside the lake that stretched the length of the park. Like Kensington Gardens, this park had once been attached to a nearby royal residence, in this case St. James's Palace.

From my vantage point, I could look across the water toward the magnificent white building known as the Horse Guards. Beyond that, the London Eye, the world's largest "Ferris" wheel, arched toward the sky. The clock tower of the Houses of Parliament loomed in its golden baroque glory next to it. The scene was postcard perfect.

The day was cooler, and the last of the bluebells decorated the edges of the sidewalks. My sandwich and tea tasted divine, and as I ate, I began to feel my strength return. It was not just physical strength but something spiritual as well. I felt more familiar to myself, more at home in my own skin.

When I raised the last bite of sandwich to my mouth, I studied my left hand. A pale strip remained at the base of my ring finger, reminding me that all evidence of my life with Edward was now gone. Well, not quite all. The sandwich demolished, I dug in my purse again, although this time not for my notebook and pen. Instead, my fingers found the side zipper pocket. I opened it and rummaged around until I found what I was looking for. I pulled out the objects and placed them in the palm of my other hand.

My wedding rings. I closed my fingers around them, weighed their lightness in my hand. Then, with a deep breath, I stood up, walked toward the water, and . . .

Stopped my arm in midmotion. Instead of flinging my

rings into the lake, I shoved them into my pocket, picked up a small stone from the bank, and tossed it into the water. It landed with a satisfying plunk and sank beneath the surface, leaving only the small ripples that undulated outward, marking where it had disappeared. In a moment, even those were gone, and the surface of the lake was as still as ever.

I returned to the bench, opened my purse again, retrieved the notebook and pen, and set to work once more.

❧❧❧❧❧

By the time midafternoon rolled around, it was a toss-up as to which was more sore, my hand from all that writing, my posterior from the wooden bench, or my brain. Writing like this was far different from dry academic scholarship. As I emerged from the trancelike state I'd been in, a thought occurred to me. While the theater might accommodate a range of apparel choices, dinner at the Ivy would require more elegance than my jeans, white button-down shirt, and cross-trainers provided. And unless I wanted to go home to Hampstead and change clothes, I was going to have to go shopping. But with what?

Almost of their own volition, my hand dug into the pocket of my jeans. My wedding rings. I hadn't been able to go through with it before, when I'd asked Adam about the pawnbrokers, but now—

It wasn't sensible. If I was going to pawn my rings, I knew I should save the resulting cash for the most absolute of emergencies—in case I got sick or couldn't find any other way to buy a plane ticket home. I certainly shouldn't use it to go on a shopping spree, or even a shopping spurt.

But behind me, across Green Park, past the Ritz and Hatchards bookshop, lay Bond Street, Regent Street, and Oxford Street. Among the three, they were home to every designer and high-end boutique known to womankind. They were filled with appropriate choices for a night out at the theater followed by dinner at the Ivy. And all available to me, if I was willing to throw out all my old notions of doing the responsible thing and indulge myself for once.

Before I could allow myself to think it through, I leaped up, discarded the remains of my lunch in a nearby trash bin, and struck out toward the biggest financial indiscretion of my life.

❧❧❧❧

Adam had told me about a high-end pawnbroker in Mayfair, and the transaction took hardly any time at all. I left the store with a purse full of cash and nerves wound tighter than a drum.

Walking was good. It calmed my nerves. I dodged middle-aged tourists in golf shirts and Rockport walking shoes, groups of schoolchildren on field trips herded along by harried-looking teachers, and lovers strolling so close together that I was amazed they could still walk when their bodies were so entwined. I made my way to Old Bond Street and its luxurious shops. Finally, I found the one I was looking for.

Chanel.

If I was going to be bad, I might as well be terrible.

The designer clothing that I'd once worn had all been selected and brought home by Edward. At the time, I thought he was an amazing husband for indulging me so extravagantly. Only after the kitchen-table day did I begin to see his indulgence as a need for control rather than a wish to please me. Consequently, I'd never been inside a designer boutique before, and I'd certainly never contemplated doing so in jeans and tennis shoes. But I'd faced the biggest humiliation I could ever encounter—the look of pity that my teaching assistant had given me over Edward's naked shoulder. She hadn't even had the grace, or the sense of self-preservation, to lower her gaze in shame. After that, what could I suffer at the hands of a snobby salesgirl that could possibly be any worse?

The front of the boutique was white, marble probably, with black trim and the simple but famous name above the door in the familiar Chanel font. I ducked inside, prepared for the worst but hoping for the best. The best being, of course, a ridiculously flattering dress that would make Barry drool, bought at a less-than-astronomical price. Even Tiffany rings could only carry a girl so far.

The sales assistant who came forward, elegantly named Jacqueline, was a sweetheart, as we would have said back home. She ushered me into the depths of the shop, seated me on a comfortable chair, and paraded a bevy of utterly gorgeous dresses before me. Silks and satins, classic and more avant-garde. After fifteen minutes, I had to shut my mouth to keep from drooling. I was too scared to ask about prices. After all, if you walked into Chanel, money should be no object.

Despite my adoration of each and every dress, though, nothing seemed quite right. And then Jacqueline produced The One.

The dress was classic Chanel. A pale pink satin slip dress covered with the sheerest black chiffon. Thin black straps that held up a gathered bodice, its rather low décolleté emphasized by the wide black satin band at the empire waist. The diaphanous chiffon skirt would graze just above my knee, while the satin underneath would feel like a sensuous second skin. It was like a black and pink Jane Austen minidress. I was in heaven, or as near to it as Chanel could take me.

Trying the thing on only made it worse. It fit perfectly, and the pink was the perfect shade for my skin tone. For the first time in almost a year, I felt pretty. Desirable. Worthy of attention. I knew that I wasn't supposed to invest my self-esteem in fashion, but when a dress made you look that good, how could you not?

"I'll take it," I said to Jacqueline when I emerged from the dressing room.

My hand trembled as I handed over the fat wad of pound notes, hoping it would be enough. I waited, held my breath, watched Jacqueline's impeccably made-up face as she counted out the money. And then she looked up and smiled at me before handing some back.

"Bien," she said and handed me the bag containing my dress. "Now, you are ready to bring him to his knees," she said with a knowing look as she escorted me to the door.

"Bring who to his knees?" I asked, startled.

"The man you are seeing tonight. You will be perfection, *non?*"

I smiled, and then I laughed. "Honestly, I just needed something for the theater—"

"Yes, yes, of course. That is what you will tell him when he sees you and cannot breathe. You are so *magnifique.*"

Every woman should get to shop at Chanel on a regular basis, I decided as I waved good-bye to Jacqueline and headed down the street. I still had other purchases to make. Shoes. Jewelry. Maybe a pashmina or shawl of some sort in case the theater or the restaurant was chilly. I hadn't done this kind of shopping, girly shopping, in a long time.

Edward had preferred me to dress in tailored, sensible clothes that I usually ordered off the Internet. But Edward was no more, and now I could make my own choices. As I made my way toward Regent Street, yet another amazing length of shops, I felt a little dizzy, like a dancer who'd been spun too many times around the floor by her partner. Like I had felt when Adam whirled me across the ballroom in Bath.

I hadn't bought the dress for him, of course. He would

never even see me in it. But Jacqueline's words, coupled with the image of Adam on his knees, didn't help to make me any steadier on my feet as I made my way through the streets of London.

he theater where *The Rivals* was playing was set just off Shaftesbury Avenue. Like most London theaters, it was old, slightly shabby, somewhat musty, and completely wonderful. From the dark paneling, the ruby-red carpets, and the gilt light fixtures to the broad steps that led up to the balconies, the whole thing reeked of culture and magic and mystery. Theater had been one thing Edward and I had seen eye to eye on.

When I approached the main doors, I saw Barry, waiting impatiently. I could tell he was impatient because he glanced at his watch three times in the fifteen seconds it took me to reach him. I wasn't even late, but if he was worried I might stand him up, I felt flattered.

And then he saw me. His jaw dropped, and the exhausting afternoon of shopping and my tired, sore feet were worth it. I'd even sneaked in a semifree makeover at one of the beauty counters at Selfridges, along with a quick visit to the salon for a blowout. The makeover had been semifree because I'd felt so guilty after the saleswoman made me look so fabulous that I had to buy something. The proceeds from my rings held up well under the strain.

"You look amazing," Barry said, his green eyes lit with pure masculine appreciation. Nothing could have boosted my ego more.

"Thanks. You look pretty spiffy yourself." He was wearing khakis and a navy blazer with a striped shirt open at the collar. No necktie for a Hemingway kind of guy. "Although won't they object at the Ivy?" I nodded toward his collar.

"They never have before," he said with a wry grin. He fished in his pocket and produced a tie, coiled neatly so it wouldn't wrinkle.

"You really got the table?"

"You doubted me?"

We both laughed, and then he offered me his arm and we headed into the theater. After ordering our drinks for the interval at the bar, we made our way to our seats. London theaters were clearly built when people were much, much smaller, so the moment we sat down, our shoulders made contact. Barry turned and smiled at me, and I was glad that my broken heart made me immune to his charms. If I'd still believed in handsome heroes, Barry could have done a number on my heart to rival Edward's performance. But for now, I was safe, I was making progress in my quest, and I felt beautiful for the first time in a long time.

I should have known better than to let my guard down.

"Excuse me." A voice to my right, a voice attached to a very nice gray pin-striped suit, interrupted my contentment. I half stood to allow the man to shuffle between my knees and the row of seats in front of me. And then I realized who the man was.

"Adam!"

He was looking at me strangely, and I'm sure I was returning the favor. I straightened to a standing position, which still left me a good half foot shorter than him.

"What are you doing here?" I asked, unable to come up with anything less clichéd.

"I could ask you the same thing."

Apparently, Adam couldn't do any better, cliché-wise. He was clean shaven and looked amazing in a suit and tie. In all our time as grad students, I had never seen him wearing anything more formal than a polo shirt. "You didn't tell me you were going to the theater tonight."

"I didn't know."

And then Adam noticed Barry sitting next to me. Barry, too, rose to his feet. "Are you a friend of Emma's? Pleasure to meet you."

They shook hands, and then Barry placed a possessive hand on the small of my back. Adam bristled. And I wanted to slide beneath the seats and slither to the nearest exit.

"I'll just take my seat." Adam squeezed past Barry and then stopped. He looked at the ticket at his hand, and then at the number on the seat. And then I heard the sound of fate locking into place. Mrs. Parrot. It had to be. She was the only other person in the world who knew where I was. And apparently she knew Adam as well, because she had to have given him the ticket.

"This is me," Adam said, gesturing toward the seat next to Barry.

"Great," Barry said, although he didn't look all that excited. "Em, you should trade with me. Sit between us."

And that's how it happened, how I came to be wedged between Barry's broad shoulder on my right and Adam's even broader one on my left, even as my mind whirled, trying to make sense of it all. I didn't need the pashmina I'd bought earlier. We were packed in like sardines, and the last thing I would have to worry about was catching a chill.

Mercifully, the house lights dimmed and the play began. I had forgotten the plot of *The Rivals*, but all it took was the opening scene to jog my memory. Jane Austen would have been quite familiar with Sheridan's play, and her family, who loved to put on theatricals of all kinds, might have enacted it in the barn for family and friends. Their love of novels, that somewhat scandalous new format in the late eighteenth century, had been exceeded only by their love of the theater.

The Rivals centered around a young heroine, Lydia Languish, who was determined to marry a poor soldier, in keeping with her rather foolish notions of romance. The hero, an army captain and the son of a gentleman, disguises himself as a lowly ensign to win her heart. Much hilarity ensues, along with mistaken identities, false suitors, and other farcical conventions. But in the end, Lydia casts aside her romantic notions of poverty and marries the wealthy Captain Jack Absolute like any woman of sense would do.

I was smiling before the principals even walked onstage. Mrs. Parrot was sending me yet another message, but as with Adam's presence, I was uncertain of its exact meaning. Had Jane Austen been like Lydia Languish, enamored of Jack Smith in part because of his impoverished state?

From the letters I'd seen so far, he had clearly been a penniless naval lieutenant hoping to make his fortune through his share of captured treasure. I knew it had been the practice at the time that if an English ship captured an enemy vessel, the spoils were divided among the crew according to rank. Many men had become gentlemen of fortune and property by such means during the course of the Napoleonic Wars. Had Jack been among them? And if not, had Jane rejected him for his lack of fortune?

I tried to focus on the play, to decipher Mrs. Parrot's meaning, but the men on either side of me proved a significant distraction. At one point, early in the first act, Barry slipped his arm around me, his hand resting on my shoulder where I was wedged against Adam. Adam shot me a sideways look, and even in the darkness, I could see his disapproval. But was his condemnation on general terms or on his own account? And what was his connection to Mrs. Parrot?

By the time intermission arrived, I was so tense that I could barely straighten my legs to stand. Thankfully, Barry was too self-absorbed to notice.

"Ready for that drink?" he said as we made our way toward the aisle. I was ready to bolt for freedom, but Adam's voice stopped me.

"If you don't mind, I'll join you since I'm on my own."

Barry shrugged. "Suit yourself. You'll have to wait at the bar, though."

"Actually, you can have my drink," I said before I could think through what I was saying. "I'm not thirsty. And I need to find the ladies' room."

I stumbled past Barry and practically ran up the aisle, trying not to bump and jostle the other patrons in my rush to escape. I moved so fast, in fact, that I made it to the restroom before all the stalls were full. I slipped inside the nearest one and locked the door behind me, shut the toilet lid and collapsed on the seat.

Why was Adam there? I thought back over the past few days. His presence in London. Running into him in South Kensington that first morning I went to Mrs. Parrot's. His willingness to drive me to Steventon, as well as to accompany me to Bath. His failure to turn up for lunch at Sally Lunn's. His own mysterious disappearances and late-nights on the computer. And finally his presence in the theater at that very moment.

A shiver ran across my bare arms. Adam must be in the hands of the Formidables too.

It all made sense. He was after the letters, just as I was. In his work on Sir Walter Scott, he could have stumbled across Mrs. Parrot, just as I had. Not easily, but it wasn't beyond the bounds of reason. Adam wasn't only a threat to my heart. He was a threat to any hope I had of restoring my career.

"No," I said. "Not again."

"Are you okay in there?" a voice said from the other side of the stall door, and I realized I'd spoken loud enough to be heard. *Great.*

"Um, yeah, I'm fine. Be out in a jiff."

A jiff? Who said *jiff* anymore? My mother, I realized with dismay. Apparently in times of stress, I turned into a fifty-something pastor's wife.

I reached for my purse, and then I paused. The second envelope. It was still in there, waiting to be read after the play. But I couldn't wait any longer.

My hands shook so badly, I could hardly open the envelope, but I managed. Slowly, carefully, I slid the paper out—a photocopy, thank goodness—and unfolded it.

LONDON, JUNE 1801

My dearest Jack,

I shall be brief—so brief, in fact, you shall suspect some other author's hand in this mischief, but as I prefer dancing to groveling, I will not linger. I was wrong, of course. Quite wrong to reject you out of hand. I care nothing for your name—Smith has served many a lesser man as well as greater ones. I have cared, I must admit, for your fortune—or lack of it. All my life, I have felt deeply my parents' struggle to feed and clothe and educate more offspring than was good for them. I have been determined not to share their fate. I convinced myself, with help from others, that fortune must have an equal role to love in marriage. But these last months with no word from you have shown me my folly. If you will be so good as to meet my family this summer in Devonshire, and if your affections and wishes remain unchanged, I shall accept your proposal with good grace and none of the ill use which you withstood on the previous occasion.

Yours, etc.,

JA

Then, written upside down between the lines at the top of the page, were these words:

You know me well enough to believe I should never marry without love. Trust that I have not departed from that path in this instance.

"Not very warm and fuzzy," I said, again aloud.

"Are you certain you're all right?" The woman's voice from the other side of the door, which had sounded concerned before, now rang with impatience.

"Fine. Yes, fine. Sorry."

I refolded the letter and put it back in my purse. So she

had loved Jack Smith, spurned his offer of marriage, and then changed her mind. She must have gone to London sometime during that summer of 1801 and either run into him there or received a letter from him. This piece of paper, or the original at least, would be enough on its own to restore my career.

"People are waiting." Clearly the woman outside the stall was almost at the end of her rope. *You aren't the only one*, I wanted to say aloud, but this time I kept my thoughts to myself.

I emerged from the stall, ignored the glares from the long line of women waiting their turn, and with a quick glance in the mirror to assure myself that I still looked like Cinderella at the ball, I hurried from the restroom.

⚜⚜⚜⚜

I found Adam standing alone near the bar on the orchestra level.

"Where's Barry?"

"He had an emergency. Had to leave." Adam looked as if butter wouldn't melt in his mouth. I was immediately suspicious.

"What kind of emergency?"

Adam shook his head. "No idea. He said something about Sophie and public transportation and then he left."

I chewed my lower lip for a second. Was Adam telling the truth? There were just enough details to be convincing, but not enough to convict him as a liar.

Before I could say anything, Adam took my hand and pulled me into a niche beside the bar. The little alcove was partially concealed by long red velvet drapes.

"We need to talk," he said. Ominous words under the best of circumstances, and Adam's frown spoke volumes. But he was right.

"What did you want to discuss?" I said, determined not to let him see how agitated I was.

"Emma, I need to know what's going on. Whatever you're doing, it's not academic research." What I was doing? I pursed my lips.

"Yes, it is research." My tone bristled, along with the rest of me. "I'm here for professional reasons."

"I've never seen anyone do research like this before. Where did you go in Bath?"

I looked away and examined the flocking on the wallpaper just past Adam's shoulder. He knew enough to be suspicious but not enough to convict me. "I had something I needed to do."

"Something secret?"

I looked him in the eye. "Why would I be doing something in secret?"

"Edward called."

I felt my eyes grow wide.

"When?"

"While we were in Bath. I picked up the message on the machine after you left this morning."

"What did he want?" Act casual. Don't flinch.

"He wants you to call him."

"What else did he say?"

Adam reached out and placed a hand on my arm. "Emma—"

"What did he say?"

"He wants you to give him a call."

I shook my head. "No."

He took a step toward me. The alcove wasn't that big to begin with, and now I was as close to him as I'd been in our seats. Only this time it was face-to-face, instead of shoulder to shoulder.

"Don't," I said, but he moved closer anyway. So close I could sense the rise and fall of his chest without looking at it.

"Em—"

"Why?" The question crawled out of my throat, scratchy and uncomfortable and totally beyond my control. "Why?" I echoed, though I knew I wasn't exactly making sense.

I didn't even care about Mrs. Parrot anymore, not when the idea of Edward's phone call felt like a knife twisting through me. Suddenly the pain was as fresh as it had been on the day I'd discovered him cheating on me. "Why did he have to do it, Adam?"

"He's an idiot, Em. He always has been."

"I'm so desirable that idiots cheat on me?"

Adam chuckled but not in an unkind way. And then his hands were on my shoulders, and then one was cradling my chin and lifting it so I had to look him in the eye.

"Edward's a lot of things. Idiot's one of his better quali-
ties. But whatever he is, Em, it's no reflection on you."

I swallowed a sob. "Of course it's a reflection on me. I was
stupid enough to marry him. To believe his shtick."

Adam shook his head, and his hand fell away from my chin.
I felt the loss keenly until he reached around and cupped his
palm across the back of my head. Holding me in place, as it
turned out, so that he could kiss me.

Some people, some people like Jane Austen, might say
that it was in bad taste to kiss a man in a public theater, even
in an alcove, but I would beg to differ. What I did know was
that despite everything that had happened, everything I'd been
through, no matter how shattered my heart had been after
Edward's betrayal or how suspicious I was of Adam having a
connection to Mrs. Parrot, I wasn't done with men. Or, for that
matter, love.

And from the way he was kissing me, I would have to guess
that Adam had a rather keen interest in it himself.

dam was still kissing me when I heard the bells. Not wedding bells. More like chimes. The ones that announced the end of the intermission, summoning Adam and me from the alcove. I stepped back and turned away from him. My cheeks were far pinker than my dress, and out of the corner of my eye, I could see that Adam was smiling as we emerged from our hiding place. I had no idea what to say to him, so I didn't say anything.

He escorted me back to our seats. Barry was gone, but the Chanel shopping bag was still there, filled with my casual clothes from earlier in the day. We had just slid into our seats when the lights dimmed.

Later, after the obligatory standing ovation and the stream of people pouring out into the London night, I still had no idea whether to bring up the subject of that clandestine kiss or just keep my mouth shut. Adam remained the same as ever, making conversation but never acknowledging what had happened between us.

I didn't exactly want to bring it up on the tube ride home. The conversation didn't need an audience. By the time we reached Hampstead, I was so exhausted, I could barely stumble up the passage to Holly Mount. Adam took the shopping bag from me with one hand and my elbow with the other, and I was thankful for his support. The night air was warm and soft, and in Hampstead, it was mostly free from the diesel fumes so prevalent in the city.

"Almost there," Adam said encouragingly as we approached Anne-Elise's town house, but then he stopped in his tracks. And so did I.

"Did you mean to leave the lights on?" I asked him. The place was lit up like a Christmas tree.

Adam stopped, frowned, and set the Chanel bag on the ground. "I didn't leave any lights on," he said.

"There's music too," I said, exhaustion giving way to concern.

We approached the front door. Adam turned the handle. It wasn't locked.

"I'll go in first," he said. I didn't waste energy arguing with him but just followed him over the threshold.

We moved down the hall to the kitchen. The music— eighties pop—emanated from there and told me what I needed to know even before we laid eyes on the unexpected visitor. Well, not a visitor exactly, since it was Anne-Elise's house, after all.

"Emma! Adam!" Her straight blond hair flew around her head as she danced around the kitchen, a tea towel tucked into the waistband of her low-rise jeans. Anne-Elise was tall, thin, and achingly beautiful. The fact that we shared any part of a gene pool had always seemed miraculous, or at least statistically improbable.

"Anne-Elise! What are you doing here?" I ran forward to give her a hug. Adam followed at a slower pace.

"I decided the two of you needed a chaperone," she said with a bright, albeit forced, smile. "So I came back from Paris early."

I caught her wrist to stop her in midtwirl and turned her to face me. "Nice try, *chérie*, but I'm not buying it. What's wrong?"

Anne-Elise stopped dancing, and in an instant, she went from bottled sunshine to Gaelic tragedy. "Etienne. I found him with another woman."

I bit my tongue to keep from offering my opinion, which was that Anne-Elise was much better off without that creepy excuse for a Frenchman. I'd met him the previous summer, at another cousin's wedding, when he'd pinched my backside repeatedly.

"When did you get back?" I asked instead.

She glanced at her watch, an expensive diamond-encrusted bauble. Probably a guilt offering from the offending Etienne. "An hour ago? Maybe two?"

Anne-Elise might have spoken with an American accent. She might even have looked like a classic California blonde. But at heart, she was her mother's daughter, and she had the charm and savoir faire of any Frenchwoman worth her *sel*.

"I have come home to seek the solace of family," she said, relishing the drama. "And of friends too," she added with an apologetic smile to Adam.

"You're better off without him," I said, not biting my tongue for long. I certainly could speak from experience.

"You're right." Anne-Elise reached for the teakettle. "I've already had three cups of tea, so I won't sleep tonight. Want to help me make it four?"

I nodded. "Sure."

What else could I say? My cousin was in need. Also, Anne-Elise's arrival meant I could avoid a potentially very awkward conversation with Adam, at least until the next day. And I had decided on the tube ride home, that I had to act as if the kiss had been nothing. Chalk it up to the heat of the moment or temporary insanity or Londonitis. Because aside from the shabby state of my own emotions, I didn't know if I could still trust him. He was in league with Mrs. Parrot somehow and hiding every bit as much as I was.

"I'm going to turn in," Adam said. He shot me a look that told me he knew exactly what I was doing, avoiding him. "I'll leave you two to your girl talk," he added, but he was looking at me when he said it. "See you in the morning."

So I wasn't going to be able to avoid the conversation forever. But at least for now, I had a reprieve.

"Do you want Earl Grey or Breakfast Blend?" Anne-Elise asked as I watched Adam disappear through the doorway.

"Whichever one is decaffeinated," I said, because unlike

Anne-Elise, I wasn't going to need tea to keep me up all night. My own bad judgment would do the trick very nicely.

❧❧❧❧❧

"So what's going on between you and Adam?" Anne-Elise was nothing if not direct. We had settled in at the table, tea at the ready.

"What do you mean?" She might be straightforward, but I had vague down to an art form.

"Don't play dumb, Emma. It doesn't suit you, especially since you got your PhD."

"It's nothing. Just a misunderstanding—"

"You snogged him, didn't you?" Anne-Elise leaned forward, her forearms braced against the table, a teasing light in her catlike green eyes.

"What?" I attempted to feign innocence.

"You know, snogged him. Kissed him." Her eyes sparkled now. She'd always enjoyed teasing me.

"I don't think—"

"Good."

"What do you mean, good? It's a disaster." I gripped my mug of tea too tightly, and the heat burned my fingers.

"Hah! So you did snog him."

"Will you quit calling it that?" I cast a nervous glance toward the door, even though Adam was long gone.

"I was hoping this would happen."

"What do you mean you were hoping it would happen?"

"When I invited you both to stay here." Now she was smiling with satisfaction.

"But Adam and I hadn't spoken in ten years. Why in the world would you think that we would—"

"Because I have eyes. And precisely because you haven't spoken in ten years. He was furious when you married Edward."

I shook my head. "He was just mad because I didn't listen to his advice."

"You're kidding, right? You think he disappeared from your life because his ego was bruised?"

"Wasn't it?"

He'd been irrationally angry with me, which had made me angry too. The last time I'd seen Adam ten years before, he'd been walking away from me after our massive argument in the middle of the Student Life Center.

"It wasn't his ego, Emma. For someone who's supposed to be a scholar, you're not very observant."

"Maybe that's why I don't have a job anymore." And then it hit me, the import of what Anne-Elise had said. "You mean you invited me to stay here so you could fix me up with Adam?"

"Why not?" There was the Frenchwoman in her. The little shrug, the smile that said, *But of course.* "Someone had to resurrect your love life."

"My love life did not need . . ." Okay, I couldn't finish that one with a straight face.

"You and Edward were never a good match."

"And you couldn't be bothered to mention that when you were my maid of honor?"

"Would you have listened?"

I paused. Swallowed. Took another sip of my tea. She wasn't the first person to ask me that very question.

"That's what I thought." Anne-Elise refilled her cup from the teapot. "No one could have talked you out of it. You were determined that Edward was your Mr. Sprightly."

"Mr. Knightley."

"Whatever." A dismissive wave of the hand. I would have to practice that a hundred times in front of a mirror to achieve the same élan. "You were so certain that you had to have a hero that you forgot to look for a man."

"What?"

"Who could measure up to your Jane Austen fantasies? No mere mortal could satisfy you."

"We were happy." My voice was softer now, and I could feel the sting of tears. My lower lip quivered. "At least, I was."

"That is all in the past," Anne-Elise said. She nodded toward my cup. "More?"

"No. I think I've drunk enough tea to float a ship since I crossed the pond."

"Only one ship? Then you definitely need to keep going." Anne-Elise splashed more tea into my cup. "Edward is the past. Another man, even if you don't want Adam, will be your future. What could be simpler?"

"Simple? You think this is simple?"

"Emma, you always did make your own complications."

"What's that supposed to mean?" Well-meaning cousinly advice was one thing, but I was starting to feel like a bug under a microscope.

"Your obsession with a happy ending. Life can't be like that."

But it could, I wanted to say. Look at my parents' marriage. After almost forty years together, my mother and father still loved each other deeply. Maybe not in the same way they had when they'd married, and it wasn't always sunshine and roses, but they loved each other, and it was still true and real. Anne-Elise's parents, on the other hand, had split up when she was ten. She'd never understood my perspective because her own life had been so different.

"I don't think there's anything complicated about finding your man with another woman," I said morosely into my tea-cup, but the statement, which previously had always pierced my heart with grief, now felt like more of a familiar ache, an old injury that hurt but didn't burn.

I looked up at Anne-Elise. "Oh, shoot, honey. I forgot."

Now her eyes were the ones filling with tears. "I suppose that our hearts get broken whether or not we believe in happy endings," she said with a sniff.

I went scurrying for a box of tissues. By the time I returned with them in hand, Anne-Elise had recovered her composure.

"So, you're not interested in Adam at all?" she asked, a measured look in her eye.

I froze for a moment, debating. I'd just told her Adam wasn't in the cards for me. I couldn't back down now.

"No. We're just friends."

"Then you wouldn't mind if I . . ." Her voice trailed off in that French way that suggested without actually stating.

"*Um*, well, no. I guess not. I mean, of course not." What was I saying? But I couldn't stop myself, and I couldn't tell her to stay away from Adam without revealing that I was struggling with my own feelings.

"As long as you're okay with it," she said and dabbed at her eyes with a tissue.

"But Etienne—" I said, hoping to remind her that she was grieving, not on the lookout for a new boyfriend.

"Is in the past." The firm set of her jaw brooked no argument. "Time to move forward. And Adam always was . . ." More shrugging and trailing off. "If you're sure you don't mind?"

And then I saw the knowing look in her eyes. I wasn't fooling anyone. Certainly not Anne-Elise, and most definitely not myself. The thought of Adam with another woman was as painful as it had been with Edward.

By the time I climbed the stairs to my room that night, it was almost three o'clock in the morning. Adam's door was shut, and no light showed beneath the door. Exhausted, I slipped on my nightgown and climbed into bed, but Anne-Elise's words kept coming back to me, holding sleep at bay.

Had I really been so busy looking for a hero that I had neglected to look too closely at the man? If I had, then it was definitely Jane Austen's fault. She had sucked me in, with her Darcys and Wentworths and Knightleys. She had tricked me into believing that such men existed.

That woman has a lot to answer for was my last thought before I succumbed to exhaustion.

espite my troubled sleep, I was awake by seven o'clock the next morning. Or, to be more accurate, I woke up when I heard the sound of footsteps in the hallway outside my bedroom. Adam was up and moving.

I don't know what instinct made me climb out of bed and throw on some clothes. I slipped into the bathroom to wash my face, brush my teeth, and try to brush my hair into some sort of order. I could only hope Adam was in the kitchen, fixing breakfast.

A few moments later, though, just as I was pulling on my tennis shoes, I heard the sound of the front door closing. Without really thinking it through, I grabbed my purse and headed after him.

I'd never stalked anyone before, either openly or in the clandestine manner I employed as I followed Adam toward the tube station. Fortunately, there was a small throng of workers heading in the same direction.

The elevators proved a bit tricky, but I managed to catch the one after his and even to lose myself in the crowd on the platform while we waited for the train. Things got easier after that. He changed at Leicester Square Station, and here the crowds made it difficult to keep up with him. Adam was tall, so I could see his head as it bobbed toward the Piccadilly line, the one that went to South Kensington, and I felt my pulse start to throb in my throat.

We boarded that train, me one car behind him, and by the time he exited at the Gloucester Road Station, I knew exactly where he was going. And when he made a beeline for Mrs. Parrot's door, I fervently wished I'd stayed in bed. Sometimes, ignorance is indeed bliss.

❧❧❧❧❧

I couldn't very well stand on Mrs. Parrot's doorstep and wait for Adam to emerge. Besides, I needed some time to think, so I kept walking, circling the block, and then finally decided to head back toward the tube station and the anonymity of a coffee shop or sidewalk café. I could keep an eye out for Adam, because he'd have to return that way to catch the tube. At least, that was my excuse. I wasn't ready to confront either him or Mrs. Parrot, not until I knew more than I did at that moment.

The tickets to *The Rivals* hadn't been a coincidence, obviously. Whatever else Adam and I might have been after the previous night, we were now competitors, and academic competition was as cutthroat as any you would find in professional sports or among Wall Street suits. Conventional wisdom said that academics were so fiercely competitive because what they fought about was so unimportant to normal people. But then, no one had ever said that academic types were normal.

How much did Adam know about my dealings with Mrs. Parrot? That thought beat in my brain like a drum. Had his interest in me the night before been real, or was he playing me, just as Edward had?

I didn't have to linger very long over my café au lait. From inside a nondescript chain coffee shop on Gloucester Road, I watched him pass by. He was indeed headed for the tube. I studied his face as best as I could in the few seconds I had him in view. Lines etched the corners of his mouth and his shoulders looked tight. Adam was normally an easygoing guy. I might not have seen him in the past ten years, but some things you don't forget. He was very unhappy about something.

I stood up, threw my cup in the trash as I exited the coffee shop, and then I faltered. What should I do? Go after Adam? Or head for Mrs. Parrot's house? The dichotomy between my personal and professional selves was never so clear to me as in that moment. I had to choose one of them. I also knew what each choice would cost me.

With a deep breath, I set out down the sidewalk, determined, this time, to do what was best for me, and not for someone else. To grab hold of my future and wrest my destiny from it.

Or, failing that, to at least figure out what in the world was going on.

❧❧❧❧❧

"Emma, dear. I thought that would be you," Mrs. Parrot said as she opened the door for me. "Let's go straight through to the lounge. I'm sure we have a great deal to discuss after last night."

If she only knew the half of it. But then, she probably did.

Her demeanor was a complete turnaround from my last visit. Then, she'd met me on the doorstep, thrust the envelopes into my hands, and sent me on my way. Now it was as if she had all the time in the world.

We went through to the lounge, and I looked around for any sign that Adam had been there. A fresh tea tray sat at the ready. No signs of previous use. The cushions on the sofa were plump and smooth. Mrs. Parrot looked cool as a cucumber.

"Did you enjoy the play?" she asked.

She proceeded to pour the tea, and my gag reflex kicked in. What was it with the British and their liquid consumption? Yes, there had been days after Edward's betrayal when I'd almost drunk my body weight in Diet Coke, but it wasn't something I could sustain over the long haul.

"I enjoyed it very much," I said, then I hesitated. Should I bring up Adam's presence? Or should I play dumb?

"You will have caught the reference, of course, to Jane Austen's own situation."

"I wasn't sure if it was meant to be literal or ironic. I know she would never have married without money to support her choice. She was pragmatic, if nothing else. But I thought perhaps . . ."

"Yes?"

"Did Jack Smith turn out to be like Captain Absolute? Did his natural father acknowledge him? Provide for him in any way?"

I was afraid I already knew the answer. If Jack Smith had been given even a modest sum, he would have carried Jane off without delay. But there had been no carrying off. At least, none that was known.

Mrs. Parrot shook her head with a smile. "We shall see."

"You already know the answer, though," I said, hoping to prod her into some sort of revelation.

"But telling you would spoil all the work you've done so far, Miss Grant."

"This really doesn't feel like work."

"But it is. Important work. You'll see that in time."

I wasn't sure I would ever see anything but what a fool I was being, running around England at the behest of a doddering, orange-haired pensioner. I had thought that all she was about was making me earn the privilege of learning "the truth," as she'd called it, about Jane Austen, but now that I knew she was also in league with Adam.

"Why me?" I said, trying to keep the frustration from my voice. "I mean no disrespect, Mrs. Parrot, but why am I here? What is it you want from me?"

"The Formidables choose whom we engage for a reason." She attempted to smile mysteriously, but it didn't quite work with that shock of flame-colored hair.

"Then what reason did you have for choosing me?" I asked, pressing her for some sort of information.

"We keep a careful eye on the scholarly community. We have to cultivate . . ." She paused. "Anyway, we heard about your . . . difficulties. We believed in your innocence."

"On what basis? You didn't know me from—" I stopped myself before I could say the name.

"That's true. But for your teaching assistant to claim authorship of that paper was absurd. Well, anyone with half a brain could see that was poppycock. That particular endeavor showed a great passion for Austen and her novels. Your teaching assistant seemed to reserve her passion for . . ." She took a sip of tea. "Well, perhaps least said, soonest mended."

"So, what are you people, the Jane Austen mafia?" Or some sort of deranged group of fairy godmothers? I didn't voice the second question aloud.

Mrs. Parrot shrugged. "We are simply protecting our interests."

"I'm one of your interests?" Yes, there was definitely more at work than my learning the truth about Jane Austen.

"Our interest does not entitle you to anything. Let me be clear on that score."

"If you would just allow me to publish a few of the letters—"

She shook her head with a sad smile. "You know we can't do that."

"Not even in this desperate a situation?" Panic clogged my throat. "Mrs. Parrot, I have no job, no home, no money. I'm desperate."

"I know, dear"—she reached over to pat my hand—"but all will turn out well in the end."

But how could it? I wanted to screech. I held myself in check, but only just.

"Mrs. Parrot—"

"Two more tasks," she said, reaching for the knitting bag at her feet. "You're making excellent progress."

Frustration joined with the panic breeding inside me. "Is all this really necessary?"

Mrs. Parrot nodded. "Yes. But we don't expect you to understand that at this juncture."

She pulled yet another of those tantalizing envelopes from the knitting bag. Oh, how I wanted to stand up, bid her good-bye, and walk away. I was tired of being someone else's puppet. Did it matter whether the person pulling my strings was Edward, Adam, or Mrs. Parrot? But even as I rebelled on the inside, I knew I couldn't go through with it. She offered me the envelope, like Eve proffering the fateful apple, and I couldn't stop myself. I took it.

"Where am I going this time?" I asked with weary resignation.

"Lyme," Mrs. Parrot said with a wink.

Easy for her to act like a co-conspirator, given that she held all the cards. Or letters, as it were.

"As in Lyme Regis?"

It wasn't really a question, but I felt compelled to ask it anyway. The resort town on the Dorset coast in southwest England held many connections with Austen and her work.

"A seaside holiday might do you some good." Mrs. Parrot picked up her knitting needles and yarn and began to stitch away as if she hadn't a care in the world. "We've taken the liberty of booking a small cottage for you."

"But—" My current budget would in no way stretch to cover those kind of accommodations.

"Our treat, of course."

Of course. I sighed.

Mrs. Parrot continued without missing a beat. "You're to read the letter on the Cobb at Lyme," she said, referring to the long stone pier that arched out into the English Channel. "And when you return to London, come and see me again."

"Mrs. Parrot—"

"I know you're weary, my dear, but please believe that there is a method to our madness."

"About Jack Smith—" I stopped myself.

I needed to know, but I also didn't want to hear the answer. Obviously, something had happened since Austen never married him. But had her heart been broken by design or fate? Betrayal or chance? I wanted to know so that I could prepare myself. Steel myself against what was coming.

I knew that for the better part of three years, from May 1801 until 1804, no letters from Austen existed, at least none that had been made public. I had a feeling, though, that when I read the letter at Lyme, I was going to discover the exact reason for her silence. I also knew, from Austen's existing letters and my own research, that she had abandoned her novel writing during that time period too. I could see the storm clouds on the horizon, but I had no idea how bad the weather was going to be.

"Don't look so glum, my dear," Mrs. Parrot said. "As I said, you're doing very well."

I swallowed the bitter laugh that rose in my throat. Mrs. Parrot must have had a rather broad definition of the phrase *very well*.

"I hope you're right" was the only response I could manage.

Twenty minutes and a second cup of tea later, I left the house, far more troubled—and waterlogged—than when I had entered. I hadn't been able to obtain the answers to any of my questions. Quite the opposite, in fact. I still wasn't sure exactly what Mrs. Parrot was about, why she and the Formidables had taken such an interest in me. And now I had no one I could trust, not even Adam. I hadn't thought it would be possible to feel lonelier than I did after Edward's betrayal, but sadly, I found that it was. Much lonelier, as a matter of fact.

didn't want to return to Anne-Elise's
house and a possible confrontation
with Adam, but I couldn't afford
another shopping spree either. So I
would have to return to Hampstead and retrieve some clothing
and toiletries for my expedition to Lyme. Or . . . wait. I could
avoid going back, I realized with a pang of relief, if I could find
someone who would do my packing for me.

I stopped at one of the iconic red phone booths on the
street, and after five minutes of trying to figure out how to
make a local call—the fact that London had eight-digit phone
numbers and more than one "area code" didn't help matters—I
finally reached Anne-Elise.

"I need you to pack me a bag and meet me in Hyde Park."

"You sound like you're in some sort of spy movie," Anne-
Elise chided me. "Just come back to the house and explain what
in the world is going on."

"I can't. You're going to have to trust me on this."

"Does it have anything to do with why Adam's stomping around like his favorite football team just lost the Super Bowl?"

I didn't answer.

Anne-Elise sighed. "I hope you two are going to be worth all this trouble in the end."

"There's no 'you two,' Anne-Elise. I think you'd better give your matchmaking efforts a rest. Besides, weren't you interested in him for yourself?"

"Yeah, right." Now she sounded like the born-and-bred American that she was. "Like I can't see the attraction emanating off the two of you in waves."

"For the last time—"

"Spare me the denials and tell me what you want me to pack."

Anne-Elise might have been a bit quirky, but she was a good friend in a tight spot. I rattled off a list of the necessities and hoped she would remember everything.

"Give me a couple of hours," she said. I was hardly in a position to bargain.

"All right. I'll see you then. At the café near the Serpentine, where we had that amazing cheesecake that time."

The wonderful thing about people with whom you shared a history is that you developed your own kind of shorthand.

"*Mon dieu*, that was incredible," Anne-Elise said, and I could envision the rapturous expression on her face. "Do you remember the raspberries—"

"Anne-Elise!"

"Okay, okay. I'm going. I'll see you in two hours."

"And don't tell Adam," I warned her before we said our good-byes.

I stepped out of the phone booth and onto the busy London street. I didn't know how I was going to occupy my time until I was supposed to meet up with Anne-Elise. Except that there was one thing I could do anywhere, really. I found a bench outside a nearby church and retrieved the notebook and pen from my purse. This compulsion was starting to scare me, but the only way to assuage it was to put pen to paper. I settled onto the bench, tuned out the din of traffic and pedestrians, and lost myself in the glide of ink across the page.

❧❧❧❧❧

To reach Lyme, I took an afternoon West Country train from London's Waterloo Station to Axminster. From there, it was a five-mile taxi ride to Lyme Regis. I had wanted to hustle to the Cobb to get my task over with, but by the time I had checked into the charming little cottage, I was too tired to do anything but collapse on the bed and fall into a deep sleep.

I awoke the next morning, lonely and depressed, but then I opened the shutters at the bedroom window and looked outside.

The cottage was situated on the Marine Parade, and the view across Cobb harbour was breathtaking. Boats bobbed in the dark blue water, and I could see the Cobb in the distance where it stretched into the sea. Low clay cliffs gave way to sandstone and beaches, and tourists abounded even during the week.

As I took in the view, I was only sorry that I wouldn't be staying longer. As soon as I completed my task, I planned to grab the next taxi back to Axminster, and from there the next train back to London.

The landlady, a Mrs. Pierpont, had left me well provisioned, I discovered, when I made my way to the little kitchen. Bread, eggs, bacon, and coffee—the staples for a hearty English breakfast. To my surprise, I was ravenous.

I indulged, frying up the eggs and bacon and broiling the toast the old-fashioned way, as my mother had done when I was a child. The fortifying meal gave me not only renewed strength but a shot of courage as well. Today, I would learn the fate of Jack Smith. I was sure of it. I only wished that, whatever it was, it had ended in a happier manner for Jane Austen.

I had slept so late that it was almost noon when I set out for the Cobb. I made my way down the Marine Parade, the beach cluttered with families and hearty individuals out for a bracing dip in the sea.

At last, I reached the harbour and made my way out onto the massive stone wall that jutted into the sea, creating a safe basin for the local boats. The long stone wall was the setting for one of Austen's most famous scenes, when Louisa Musgrove of *Persuasion* jumped from the higher level of Cobb instead of using the steps, expecting Captain Wentworth to catch her. His failure to do so, and her resulting injury, binds him to her as surely as if he'd offered a proposal of marriage. And it kills the hopes of the novel's long-suffering heroine, Anne Elliott, who had been persuaded eight years before to refuse the marriage offer of the very same promising but impecunious captain.

Now, two centuries later, sea spray splashed against the stone, and the bracing salt air filled my lungs until they almost burned. Seagulls, hoping for a few morsels from the tourists, circled overhead.

I walked out a good fifty yards, until there was nothing around me but the sea and the wind and the sun. I could easily imagine Jane Austen walking there during one of her family's seaside stays, filled as I was with a sense of peace and magnificence and even freedom. Two of her brothers had been navy men. From the descriptive passages in her novels, especially *Persuasion*, I knew she shared their love of the ocean. Perhaps it was on this very spot she had first imagined Captain Frederick Wentworth, the hero of her final novel.

The barren rock didn't offer a place to sit, so I took the letter out of my purse and clutched it in the face of the rather stiff breeze. I was about to unfold it when I heard a voice calling my name.

"Emma!"

I turned, and my heart leaped into my throat. The last place

I had expected to encounter Edward again was on the Cobb at Lyme Regis.

⚜⚜⚜

"I can't believe you're here." My feet rooted themselves in the stone beneath my feet.

Edward was smiling from ear to ear, his salt-and-pepper hair ruffled by the sea breeze. He was a handsome man, and despite everything, I felt that old tug of attraction. I'd always found him compelling. That hadn't changed.

"Adam told me where to find you. I saw you go past on the Parade, but I couldn't catch you in time." He stood there like something out of a dream, dressed in khakis and a lightweight anorak, just as I'd seen him a thousand times before.

But Adam had sent him? How had he known where I was, unless Anne-Elise had broken her word? I wasn't sure how to interpret this strange turn of events. Adam could have sent Edward as a sign that I should try to repair my marriage. Or he could have sent him to find me so I could put the past to rest and move forward.

"What do you want?"

His smile faded, and I was pretty sure I understood the lines of contrition that marked his face. For whatever reason, he had come to try and reinstate himself in my good graces. He had a sheepish look about him that was distinctly un-Edward.

"I made a mistake, Emma. A number of them, to be honest."

The water pounded against the Cobb, sending a fine spray into the air that covered us without drenching hair or clothing.

"Yes, I'm aware of that." I could keep the irony out of my voice but not out of my words. It was strange how calm I felt, in spite of the adrenaline pouring through my body.

"I'd like to try again. I want to make it up to you." He reached for my hand, and I let him take it. "Chalk it up to a midlife crisis, or male stupidity, but I'm over that now. I see things much more clearly. I know what a fool I've been."

"So do I, Edward."

A few months earlier, I would have received his apology very differently. Now I withdrew my hand from his grasp. Another wave, this one even larger, crashed against the stone, nature's innate attack on human intrusion. Now the spray was much stronger, misting my shirt and dampening my hair. "The problem is much more than our marriage."

"But if we can go back to the way we were—"

"You helped ruin my career," I snapped. "I'm not sure my better nature stretches to forgiving you for ruining me both personally and professionally."

He had the good grace to blush. That red stain across his cheek looked pretty strange, but I found it somewhat satisfying. I wanted him to feel the kind of shame he'd inflicted on me.

"I honestly thought—"

"You're a liar, Edward. You always were."

My barb struck home. Edward bristled. "I said that I was

sorry, Emma. And I'll take my punishment, but I won't stand here and let you browbeat me."

"Are you serious?" I stepped back. My hands landed on my hips. "Are you in any way serious?"

"I don't see how demeaning me will make up for the damage that's been done to you," he said. He moved forward, trying to draw me back into the circle of his charm. "What good can come of exposing my lapse in judgment?"

"So your idea of atonement is that I take you back, don't demand that you clear my good name, and what? What else, Edward? Would you like the moon and the stars as well as the sun?"

"It's not like you were the picture of perfection, Emma. You contributed to the difficulties in our marriage as much as I did." He wiped his tousled hair out of his eyes.

The longer hairstyle should have been one of the first signs that Edward's affections had strayed. That and his sudden need to do sit-ups every night to flatten his stomach.

"My shortcomings?" I gasped.

Evidently, loving the man you married and trusting him beyond anyone else was now a character flaw. Although, to be fair, when it came to my faith in Edward, that had been a critical error of judgment on my part, indeed.

"Emma, just forget this foolishness and come home with me. We'll sort it all out." He paused. "I love you."

I looked at him, the sun exposing every wrinkle and age

spot on his face. One upon a time, I'd thought him handsome in a mature, worldly way. Now, he just looked old.

"Why are you here?" Suspicion, my constant companion since the fateful kitchen-table incident, made herself known. "Why now?" Red flags were popping up in my mind's eye like poppies after rain.

"I know I've given you plenty of reason not to trust me—"

"Someone's uncovered your lie, haven't they? Or at least your part in it?"

He blanched, the color draining from his face as suddenly as it had come over him, and I knew I was right.

I laughed, not out of joy but out of vindication. "Someone caught you with your hand in the cookie jar. How much trouble are you in, Edward, for championing a lying teaching assistant over your own wife?"

He paused, swallowed, licked his lips. Then he reached into the inside pocket of his jacket and withdrew a sheaf of folded papers.

"I need your signature on this," he said, and I could tell he was trying to muster his dignity.

My hand shook when I took the papers from him, but I wasn't sure whether the trembling came from trepidation or satisfaction. I had dreamed of this moment, even though I'd known there was little chance of it ever happening. But when I opened the folded papers and saw the university logo on the letterhead, I knew that Edward had met his match. I might not have been able to bring him down on my own, but you could never underestimate the power of a university that wanted to avoid public embarrassment.

"They want you to sign this, saying that you won't sue for defamation of character, or libel or slander or anything along those lines." He paused. "They've also offered to admit their error publicly and reinstate you on the faculty. With an increase in salary, of course."

Such an offer could only have meant one thing—the university knew I had a successful legal claim on my hands. I didn't need to read the pages themselves. Edward's demeanor told me all I needed to know. I refolded the papers and slipped them into my purse before draping the strap back over my shoulder.

"I'll look them over. Consult an attorney."

Edward shook his head. "I promised I would bring those back with me tomorrow. Signed."

"You're leaving? So soon?" I wanted to mock him, to pour out the malice I was feeling like a poisonous fountain, but then I stopped myself. Because stooping to Edward's level would only mean that I had stooped to Edward's level. And that was one place I refused to go.

"I'll let you know," I said instead, and I took a step to move past him. He caught my shoulder.

"Don't be a fool, Emma. We can both come out of this

okay. But you have to cooperate. If you bring me down, I'll take you with me."

I laughed, because, honestly, he sounded like the villain in an old Vaudeville sketch.

"Be my guest," I said. Because in that moment, I knew how I could extricate myself from the entire mess. The answer was right there, in my purse. Everyone around me was relentlessly pursuing their own self-serving agendas. Who was I to fight city hall?

"Good-bye, Edward," I said, and I walked past him with my head, if not my heart, held high.

"You're being ridiculous!" he called after me, but I let his words slide away on the wind. "You'll regret this."

I'd come to England for a reason. I wanted to vindicate myself and expose Jane Austen for the fraud she was. But now that I knew she'd had true love in her grasp, and for whatever reason, she'd turned it away, I knew what I had to do. It was time the world knew the truth. It was time I learned the truth. And it was time I gave up my foolish, romantic notions of happily-ever-afters. Barry had been right. Women never thought beyond the happy ending. We'd been taught to believe that our world revolved around securing a commitment from a man.

Edward, Adam, Mrs. Parrot, Jane Austen—anyone who stood in my way would have to understand that I wasn't going to be a patsy anymore. The time had come to stand on my own

two feet. The world deserved to know the truth about Jane
Austen, just as it deserved to know the truth about Edward.

I marched across the length of the Cobb toward the beach.
If I was in the right, I could claim the moral high ground, but
if I had vindication and validation at my fingertips, I wondered
how I could still feel so desperately unhappy.

had wanted to read the letter on the Cobb as Mrs. Parrot instructed, but the nearby beach would have to suffice. At least I could find a bit more shelter from the wind than I could out on the pier. I made my way across the sand and found a place to sit in the midst of the tourists. At least this way I would blend into the crowd. If Edward returned, I would be difficult to spot.

My hands were surprisingly steady, given what I'd just gone through. This letter was longer than the others, I noted— two full pages of Austen's even script. And as with the others, the photocopies were a bit fuzzy in places, but I puzzled my way through.

The letter had been written by Jane from London to Cassandra, who was at Godmersham in Kent on one of her many missions of mercy to help her brother Edward and his wife, Elizabeth, with their growing brood of children. The letter contained no pleasantries. Instead, Austen presented the news in a straightforward and immediate manner. Certain phrases, though, leaped off the page and set my pulse to thrumming.

> *... as I had just determined to make him the happiest of men ...*
>
> *... now I must be the unhappiest of women ...*

My heart in my throat, I continued reading.

> *The ship sank not a day out from Portsmouth. My pen impresses the fact upon this page, yet my heart does not feel its truth. Or perhaps my mind will not comprehend such information. His fortune and my heart, along with life and limb, now lie at the bottom of the sea. How shall I look upon the scenes that I have loved—indeed, that we viewed and loved together? Sidmouth, Dawlish, even Southampton and Lyme shall be haunted for me.*

I looked up toward the sea and the dark blue line of the horizon, and then I glanced at the date at the top of the page. September of 1801. Austen had written it during the early part of the long gap in her letters, the beginning of a silence of almost four years. This letter, then, explained the disappearance of the others, for if indeed Austen's relationship with Jack Smith had been known only by Cassandra, her sister would have excised all references to him and to Jane's loss. And she had been so thorough that none of the letters had been seen by any eyes but her own, until she created the Formidables.

The news of Jack's death, if I could even call it news, given that it was more than two hundred years old, ripped a low moan of grief from my throat. The loss was not unexpected. I knew that something had happened to end their relationship. And in a way, I was relieved that Jack hadn't turned out to be a Willoughby or a Wickham, or like my Edward, for that matter. Still . . .

I dropped the pages into my lap, careful to keep a hand on them so they wouldn't be carried off by the wind. I sat there on the beach for a long time, contemplating the magnitude of the document. Even if it was only a copy, the information it contained was cataclysmic for any Austen scholar. Had Adam seen it yet? I wondered. And how would I hide my new knowledge from him when I returned to Hampstead?

Despite the warmth of the day, I started to shiver. I didn't want to think too much about the contents of the letter. Better to focus on the thing as an object in and of itself. If I thought about the emotional import, I might feel it too deeply. Jane Austen had loved a man but turned down his offer of marriage because she feared living a life of poverty. Later, she had regretted her decision and wrote to him to indicate her change of heart. He had been delighted and told her he would renew his proposal. They had planned to meet, to marry.

And then he had died. Just like that. She was left alone,

single, and as poor as she'd feared being if she had married imprudently.

I gave a half sigh, half hiccup and reached up to touch my cheek. I hadn't realized I was crying.

❧❧❧❧❧

Later, after I was sure Edward had left, I made my way back toward the cottage Mrs. Parrot had rented for me. I bypassed its blue front door, though, in favor of heading for the landlady's office. Edward's appearance and this most recent letter had snapped something within me. I had held on to my antiquated notions of romance and true love for far too long. It was time now to be practical.

I stuck my head around the door where Mrs. Pierpont was working in her cluttered warren of an office.

"Do you have a photocopier?" I asked.

A guilty flush stained my cheeks, although why I was having that reaction now, when Mrs. Pierpont had no idea what I was up to, I didn't know. Then again, for all I knew, the older woman could have been one of *them*. An undercover Formidable. I didn't want to be paranoid, but I also wouldn't have put it past Mrs. Parrot. She had booked the cottage, after all.

"I think this new printer might do that," she said, nodding toward a monstrous piece of office equipment that occupied the corner of her large mahogany desk. "You're welcome to try."

Fortunately for me, the printer wasn't too different from the one I had at home. I retrieved the envelope from my purse, took out and unfolded the letter, and laid the first page on the glass face of the scanner. I closed the lid, and with one touch of a button, I betrayed Mrs. Parrot. The machine hummed and whirled, and a few seconds later, it rolled out the evidence of my duplicity.

"Did it work?" Mrs. Pierpont asked. She seemed so vague, so uninterested despite her polite question, that I could only hope that meant she wasn't a Formidable, after all.

"Perfectly," I said, though I felt far from perfect inside.

But now that I had turned down Edward's plea to resurrect our marriage, as well as brushing aside his help in righting my career, I needed some kind of insurance, or at least some evidence that I hadn't completely lost my mind.

I copied the second page of the fateful letter, my pulse thrumming in my throat, but Mrs. Pierpont didn't seem to notice me at all.

"Thank you," I added as I put the pages in my purse and waved good-bye to her. She looked up from her account book, returned my wave with a vague smile, and resumed whatever she'd been doing when I entered the room.

Clearly, she wasn't aware that I had just turned myself into the very cheat that Edward had once accused me of being.

⚜⚜⚜⚜⚜

When I returned to Hampstead late in the day, it was all I could do to screw up my courage and walk through Anne-Elise's front door.

"Anyone home?" I called as I made my way through the center hallway toward the kitchen, hoping I would be greeted with silence.

"I'm in here," Adam answered. I stepped into the kitchen and willed myself to act with a nonchalance I couldn't feel.

"Hey," I said. He was sitting at the large farmhouse table, papers spread out from one end to the other. "More research?"

"Yes." He was polite but distant. "How have you been?"

Okay, he wasn't distant at all. He was angry. "Fine," I said and wished I had tiptoed upstairs instead of calling out.

"And Lyme Regis?"

I couldn't pretend anymore. "Why are you mad at me?"

He threw down the pen he'd been holding. "You take off yesterday without a word to anyone and don't come home last night, and you wonder why I'm angry?"

"But you knew I was—" I stopped. "Wait a minute. How did you know where I was? You sent Edward." But of course he was in league with Mrs. Parrot. He had to be, to have known where I'd gone.

Adam snorted. "Anne-Elise finally told me when I threatened to call your parents to see if they knew where you'd gone."

"And you sent Edward."

"Yes."

"Why?"

"Would you rather I hadn't?"

I didn't know what to say to that. "I don't know," I answered honestly.

Adam craned his neck and looked past me toward the hall-way. "Is he here?"

"What?"

"Didn't Edward come back with you?"

I was too shocked to be immediately insulted, although it didn't take long for my ire to follow. "Thanks a lot."

"He came crawling back on his knees, complete with papers reinstating you at the university. What more could you want?"

"Adam—"

"I have to admit, at first I thought of telling him you were in the Outer Hebrides, or whatever remote Scottish outpost I could think of."

My heart twisted in my chest at his words. Adam was most definitely jealous. That thought shouldn't have pleased me quite so much. After all, I was a modern woman who, in the-ory, believed in straightforward communication and honesty in relationships. But the look on Adam's face . . . It was as if he didn't know whether to kiss me or shun me. I had to admit it was pretty thrilling.

"I don't know where Edward is," I said and leaned against the doorjamb.

"For real?"

"For real."

That silenced him for a long moment.

"So you came back."

"Well, all my stuff is here."

"Touché." He managed that self-deprecating smile I had always found so charming. "I guess I deserved that."

"Adam . . ." I needed to ask him about Mrs. Parrot, but suddenly I was afraid, far more afraid than I'd been when Edward had shown up on the Cobb offering me everything I ever wanted on a platter.

"Yesterday . . ." My courage failed me for a moment. I couldn't ask him about the letters. I tried again. "The other night, at the theater . . ." No, that wasn't any better.

What would Jane Austen have done?

"This came with the mail today," Adam said, pulling an envelope from beneath the plethora of papers in front of him. "Sorry. Didn't mean for it to get lost in the shuffle."

I took the envelope—the dear, dratted, familiar Mrs. Parrot envelope—and held it at the edges like a photograph I was afraid to smudge.

"Today?" I said, echoing him.

"Who's it from?" Adam asked.

I looked up from the envelope into his carefully bland expression. And I knew, at that moment, that he was lying. Not with words, really. But with feigned innocence. I couldn't prove it empirically, but every fiber of my being told me that Adam knew exactly whom the letter was from.

I glanced back down, gave a small smile that was more of a grimace. "Old friend of my mother's, I think."

And then, when I lifted my gaze to his, I could see that he

knew I was lying as well. The deceit hung there between us, almost palpable. And when I couldn't bring myself to speak, it seemed to grow until it filled the room.

"I think I'll just go and . . . read it," I finished lamely. I was still standing just inside the kitchen doorway, and we were only a few feet apart. But there might as well have been an ocean between us.

"Adam—"

"I have to finish this tonight," he said, dismissing me as effectively as if he'd had me bodily escorted from the room. We weren't going to discuss any of it. Not Mrs. Parrot. Not Jane Austen's letters. Not the kiss that had rocked my world.

"Okay, then," I said, stalling even as I knew that the moment for revelation had passed. "I'll just go read . . ." I waved the envelope. "My letter," I finished lamely.

"See you," Adam said. He picked up his pen and shuffled some of his papers. "Anne-Elise and I are going to get some dinner when she gets back. You're welcome to come with us."

"Sure," I said, and I even managed not to let the sob that caught in my throat escape. "That would be great."

I spun on my heel and made as dignified an exit as I could. Even after I had mounted the stairs and sought the solace of my room, I couldn't believe the conversation—or the lack of it. Hadn't I learned anything in the debacle with Edward? Or from Jane Austen's procrastination? Or even, heaven help me, from Mrs. Parrot? Why couldn't I lay my heart on the line with Adam?

I threw myself on the bed and clutched the bolster, a hard, polelike pillow that some strange Europeans actually slept on. In my case, all it was good for was soaking up my tears.

I couldn't believe that after everything that had happened, I was still as big a wimp as the day I'd found Edward on my kitchen table. And suddenly I knew. It wasn't Jane Austen who had ruined my life.

It was me.

y now, I was utterly sick of the British railroad system. Still, after the previous days' events, I didn't dare ask Adam to drive me to Chawton, the site of my last task from Mrs. Parrot.

The station at Alton, just beyond Basingstoke, was tiny, but it was the nearest one to the cottage where Austen had spent the last years of her too-short life. There, settled with her mother and sister, she began to write again. Somehow, she found her pen and her voice once more. I could only hope that the letter in my purse would give me some clue as to how she had accomplished it, and how I could apply the lesson to my own life.

❧❧❧❧❧

In December of 1804, on Jane Austen's twenty-ninth birthday, her great friend Madame Lefroy was killed when she fell from her horse while riding. A month later, Jane's father died at the age of seventy-four. His death flung his widow and spinster daughters into true poverty.

The Austen brothers promised to do as much for their mother and sisters as they could, and indeed they offered some financial support. What they did not provide for the three dependent women was a home of their own. From the time Jane was twenty-nine until she was thirty-four, her itinerant household either stayed with relatives or occasionally took cheap rented lodgings in Bath or a seaside town.

Jane and Cassandra, the maiden aunts, found themselves much in demand by their brothers' families. Their presence must have been desired for affectionate reasons, but there were functional ones as well. Their brother Edward Austen Knight and his wife had eleven children and were always in need of an extra pair of hands. James, their oldest brother, was widowed and left with a three-year-old daughter, whom Cassandra and Jane doted on.

Mrs. Austen, Cassandra, and Jane remained rootless until the summer of 1809, when they at last arrived in the village of Chawton, Hampshire, not many miles from Steventon and the rectory where Jane had grown up. The cottage was part of an estate inherited by Jane's brother Edward, who had been adopted by wealthy relatives.

As the taxi made its way from Alton to Chawton, I could see why, if nothing else, the bucolic countryside might have proved some inducement to Austen to take up her pen again. Even now, with growth and modernization, it had retained its charm.

The taxi driver let me out in front of the solid, rectangular, red-brick cottage in the middle of the village. The house sat almost on top of the road at a place where the blacktop divided—heading in one direction for Chawton Great House, Edward's home, and in the other for Winchester and points farther west.

I had arrived in the late morning on a weekday, but already the tourists and literary pilgrims had made their presence known at Jane Austen's house. The entrance was tucked on the side, adjacent to a beautiful garden that was separated from the road by a hedge, a sidewalk, and a strategically placed bench. I joined the small queue of people ducking through the low doorway into the museum.

Jane Austen's House Museum was staffed by volunteers. A small vestibule gave way to the sitting room, which still looked much as it would have appeared in Austen's day—except for the large table in the center that displayed some of the gift items available for purchase. I approached the woman seated behind the cash register in the corner, paid my entrance fee, and began to look around.

The last envelope from Mrs. Parrot had included the instruction *Open This* on the back, and I had done so in the privacy of my room in Hampstead. Her instructions had been simple, but still I had balked. This task, in some ways, would be the most difficult of the six, but I was still determined to persuade her to give me access to the letters, so I persevered.

I squared my shoulders and slowly walked the perimeter of the sitting room, pausing to admire the pianoforte as well as the Regency costumes on dressmakers' dummies near the fireplace. I couldn't maintain my feigned interest for long, though. I stepped through the open doorway on the opposite side of the room, bypassed the small alcove that had at one time been the main entrance to the cottage, and passed through to the dining room.

A large window occupied the street side of the room, its numerous panes allowing for an expansive view. The size of the opening meant that not only did the room's occupants enjoy a great deal of light with their meals, but they would also have been among the first to see the mail coach whiz by.

A sturdy dining table and chairs took precedence in the center, and the far wall held a fireplace flanked by cabinets. But it was the window that held my interest. That, and the small table and lone chair that were drawn up next to it. These two objects were roped off, and as I stepped closer, I could see a small sign on the table.

Do not touch.

I turned and pretended to admire the china on the dining table with its gold lozenge pattern, as well as the pleasant proportions of the room. Two elderly women entered behind me, and I loitered until they moved on, through the other side and into the area that had once been the kitchen but was now the gift shop.

I stepped toward the table, only to stop in my tracks when I heard someone else enter the room behind me. Again, I circled the room, pretending to study its contents. More china. The wallpaper, even. Who would have thought that the little cottage would have been so popular?

Finally, a good fifteen minutes later, I had the room to myself. Quickly, I stepped toward the window and looked down.

It was just a plain little occasional table that looked like something you would pick up at a yard sale. I thought of her writing desk in the British Library and could envision the wooden box fitting perfectly on top of the table. Heart in my throat, I glanced over my shoulder. No one was coming. With one quick swipe, I reached over and ran my finger across the very edge of the wood.

I expected alarm bells to go off or some stern-faced volunteer to materialize and haul me off by the collar, but nothing of the kind happened. Instead, I felt a warm glow spread across my skin, like a life force I'd captured with my clandestine act. Gentle tears, softened by the sorrow and struggle of the past few months, slid down my cheeks. After reading the letter at Lyme, I had thought that coming to Chawton would depress me further, but there was a kind of peace here. A sense of rightness and of rest, as if a bit of Austen still lingered.

Here, at this table, Jane Austen had risen from the ruins of her life like a phoenix from the ashes. She'd written or rewritten almost all of her novels on this tiny bit of wood, at this wonderful window overlooking a busy village street. In the room behind her, family members and servants had traipsed back and forth. No splendid isolation or idyllic solitude for her.

In spite of all the distractions, she'd created her masterpieces with nothing more than paper, pen, and ink. Virginia Woolf was famous for saying that any woman who wanted to be a writer needed to have five hundred pounds a year and a room of her own. Austen had possessed neither of those things, and yet somehow she had outshone authors with far more worldly advantages.

"Miss?" A volunteer's voice tore me from my thoughts. I quickly wiped away my tears with the back of my hand.

"Yes?"

"I'm sorry. But we're closing early today."

"Early?"

She glanced at her watch. "I'm afraid so." And then she smiled kindly. "You're not the only one, you know. Happens quite often, in fact," she said, gesturing toward my tear-stained cheeks.

I returned her smile with a watery one of my own. "Thank you. That helps."

❦❦❦❦❦

You would have thought that the near-mystical experience of the writing table would have made me rethink the course I had set for myself on the beach at Lyme, but you would have been wrong. Jane Austen of all people would have understood that a woman had to do what a woman had to do, even if it didn't always worked out as she'd planned.

I slipped out of the cottage into the well-tended garden and spied a bench in the far corner. The grass was springy beneath my feet, the air thick with pollen and the perfume of the flowers. I fell onto the bench with a grateful sigh. I hadn't been in England that long, but at that moment, it felt like a lifetime since I'd arrived.

My hands no longer trembled when I unfolded one of the letters. Her handwriting, more familiar now, was easier to decipher. The contents, though, continued to amaze and thrill me. This time, the tone of the letter was reflective. It had been written in 1817, near the end of Austen's life, and was addressed to her sister, Cassandra, who'd been in London visiting their brother Henry.

. . . These years, snug in our cottage, have taught me that had I home and husband of my own, I should not have birthed my novels. If nieces and nephews so occupy one's time, I can scarcely imagine how as a mother I should have two moments together to call my own. My writing box and my little table by the window have been the happiest of endings. You, dearest sister, will know the truth of it, but others who know me less may not comprehend. I beseech you, take the scissors to all the letters that

might be used against me. If that task proves too onerous,
burn them or contrive to conceal them however you see fit.
Whatever you do, protect my children from the coarse and
vulgar speculations of others. The world may know my
words, but it has no such privileges with my heart.

My breath caught in my throat, the words an echo of what Mrs. Parrot had recited to me at our first meeting. What could be plainer than that? Cassandra had acted under her sister's direct request. The letters that had been made public were carefully chosen not to detract from Austen's novels. The other letters, especially the ones that had been replete with Jack this and Jack that, had disappeared from memory.

Judging from the very few I had read, no one who encountered them could ever doubt the state of Jane's heart. The Tom Lefroy letters, I realized, the ones Cassandra had made public, were a ruse, a masterful misdirection worthy of the best illusionist. And the work of the Formidables had been formidable indeed, so well had they kept their secret.

I looked up at the entrance to Chawton Cottage, at the stream of departing visitors who still lingered despite the volunteers' best efforts to disgorge them from the house. If Cassandra Austen hadn't done her sister's bidding, would Jane Austen's admirers have flocked to this remote location? Or would she have been dismissed as a thwarted spinster who continually tried to re-create her own lost love?

The truth was that a woman's romantic life could always be

used to discount her professional one. In this case, Austen must have known that her failed romance would have been used to poison the response to her novels. Circumstances, not inclination, had prevented her from marrying. She had loved and lost, and then she had chosen not to take that risk again. Instead, she had taken it on the page, which in its way, required far more courage.

I thought of her last novel, *Persuasion*, the tale of a young woman who refuses the proposal of an equally young sea captain. She is persuaded by others that she cannot be so imprudent as to overlook his lack of fortune. Eight years later, he reappears in her life, rich now from the spoils of the war but clearly still bearing a grudge from her refusal. In the course of the novel, the heroine learns to stand on her own two feet and to make her own decisions. The hero learns to forgive her for her rebuff. And, in the end, they are reunited and can build a life together.

I knew, from this last letter, that Austen came to terms with the choice she had made. She found her way in the world, and though her life had not been what her more youthful self would have dreamed, it had been unmistakably, irrevocably hers. When it came to her choices, some had been rewarded, while others had thwarted her hopes and dreams. She followed her own path to the best of her ability, and in that, she was no different from any other woman who had ever lived, or ever would.

"You've been sitting here quite a while." The familiar voice startled me. Suddenly Barry was there next to me on the bench.

"Where did you come from?" I glanced around. "How did you know I was here?"

He shrugged. "Great minds think alike, I guess. Sophie wanted to visit the Jane Austen house before we left for the Continent."

I didn't believe him. Hadn't he told me he was only in London for a few days?

"Who are you?" I scooted away from him as far as the small bench would allow. "Why are you following me?" If I'd ever thought him attractive, now I just found him creepy.

"Emma—"

"This has all been a setup, hasn't it? What were you, like, stalking me in Hampstead that first time?"

"I wouldn't say stalking. More like . . . anticipating."

I stood up. "Do not follow me," I ground out between clenched teeth, but my instructions didn't do any good. He leaped up and fell into step beside me.

I walked toward the street and then stopped. It was not a good idea to leave a populated area when you were trying to ditch a crazy man.

"I can explain," Barry said, but at least he had enough sense not to grab my arm to try and stop me. "Give me three minutes."

I glanced at my watch. "I'll give you one. And it starts now."

He ran a hand through his floppy surfer-dude hair and made it stand on end. Somehow, that rooster comb made me feel instantly better. It was hard for a man to appear menacing when his hair was sticking straight up to the sky.

"I'm aware of your . . . endeavor," he said at length.

"You have forty seconds left," I replied.

"I can help you." He crossed his arms over his chest. "And you can help me. I thought we could come to a mutually agreeable . . . well, agreement."

"Very erudite. Especially for a Hemingway scholar," I snapped.

"I really am a professor. You can look me up on the university Web site."

Too late. I already had, the first time I met him, which was the only reason I wasn't calling for a constable at that very second.

"You have twenty seconds left," I said.

"I can help you." The words came out on a rush of breath. Barry dropped his arms, but his hands clenched into fists at his side. "I can get you the help you need to publish what you have."

"Excuse me?" Okay, maybe I should have rethought that whole calling the constable issue.

"You need to publish those letters. You know better than anyone how much your reputation will gain if you do. And I represent a certain . . . consortium, shall we say, who are also interested in seeing Austen's letters come to light."

"Who? Name names."

"I can't."

I looked at my watch. "Your time's up." I turned to walk away.

"We'll pay you as well. A hundred thousand dollars."

That stopped me in my tracks. I looked at him. "Are you serious?"

"Let me see one of the letters," he said. "Then we can talk business."

I couldn't believe it when I reached in my purse and pulled out the envelope, but for a woman who'd been scraping by on change she found under the couch cushions for the last few months, an amount with that many digits was beyond temptation.

"This is it." I unfolded the letter and held it up for him, but I kept it well beyond his reach.

"Just let me—"

"No. You can look at it from there."

He grimaced. "That's not the original."

"It's a photocopy."

His shoulders sagged. "I'm sorry, but it has to be the original. A copy's worth nothing to us." He paused. "But I'll reiterate my offer. If you can produce original letters, we'll allow you to have all the credit of discovery and publication, and we'll pay you the money I mentioned."

"What are you, part of a rival literary gang or something?"

His answering smile was both self-satisfied and unctuous. "You might say that."

Great. Not only did Austen have her Formidables, but apparently Hemingway also had his own gang of thugs. Well, not thugs, but smarmy professors, anyway.

"I don't know." I looked around, suddenly worried that an unknown Formidable might be watching the whole exchange. "I'll have to think about it."

"There's nothing to think about." He leaned forward and said in a low voice, "Don't tell me you weren't already planning to publish them."

The flush that covered my cheeks actually burned. I couldn't even deny it.

"That's what I thought." He reached into the inside pocket of his navy blazer and pulled out a business card. "Here's my number and my e-mail address. Let me know what you decide."

To my eternal shame, I took it from him.

"But don't wait too long," he said with a nauseating wink. "It's not like you're our only option."

Adam. Had he managed to get Mrs. Parrot to part with some of them already? I remembered him pulling that last envelope from beneath the piles of papers on Anne-Elise's table. Had he been hiding it from me? And if so, why had he changed his mind and produced it?

"I'll let you know." That was all I could manage. And then I took off, practically running down the street. I had no idea where I was going. I only knew that I had to run away as fast as I could. The problem was, the person I most wanted to run away from was myself.

As always, Adam's note was short and sweet.

Meet me at Kenwood.

I thought it was rather optimistic of him, considering that I hadn't told him where I was going or what time I would be back. But then again, if he was in league with Mrs. Parrot, he no doubt knew precisely where I'd been all day. I could picture him at Kenwood, lying on a blanket on the vast lawn. Our picnic there seemed a lifetime ago.

Anne-Elise wasn't home either, and her note was equally succinct where she'd scribbled it beneath Adam's.

Just do it, she'd urged. Clearly she'd left after Adam and thought I would need some encouragement.

Leave me alone. That's what I wanted to write in the remaining space at the bottom of the page, but there was no one to read the message—except me.

I stood in the middle of Anne-Elise's kitchen and contemplated my choices. The easiest course would have been to avoid Adam altogether until I could get my hands on Mrs. Parrot's letters. If I went upstairs to my room, or if I took off for parts unknown, I could have saved myself a lot of heartache. Okay, not saved, but definitely postponed. Denial usually worked as a short-term strategy.

I glanced at my watch. It was almost six o'clock. By the time I changed and hiked to Kenwood, it would be at least seven. Maybe it wasn't too late, though.

Who was I kidding? It had been too late for me and Adam from the moment I'd agreed to marry Edward. Or at least from the moment I'd told Adam I had agreed to marry Edward.

A little closure wouldn't hurt, I tried to convince myself. Meeting Adam and breaking off with him formally would be the mature thing to do. It was the logical course, not a desperate attempt to squeeze in one more night of his company before I betrayed my solemn promise to the Formidables.

I dashed upstairs and pulled on the one summery dress I'd brought. The time had come to say good-bye to Adam, to make sure our relationship came to an end, because I wouldn't be able to bear the look in his eyes once he found out what I'd done.

No matter how much I tried to convince myself that he was my rival in the race to lure Mrs. Parrot into surrendering the letters, I couldn't do it. Adam just wasn't that kind of guy. Whatever his relationship with Mrs. Parrot might be, I couldn't believe he was planning to blow the lid off her conspiracy.

Unfortunately, I had discovered that under the right circumstances, I was the kind of girl to do just that.

I mounted the stairs, determined to dress, coif, and make myself up as I'd never done before.

❦❦❦❦❦

An hour later, as I climbed the last slope toward Kenwood House, I regretted the summer-dress-and-sandals decision. I hadn't thought about what a hot, dusty walk it would be. I cast a longing glance at the lake at the foot of the slope. Sadly, it was not meant for public bathing, so I soldiered on.

After much huffing and puffing, I finally gained the higher ground and the gravel walk that ran parallel to the house. Like the last time I was there, the slope was covered with picnicking couples and families. That evening, though, an orchestra had set up on the flat area near the house. I studied the crowd, feeling vulnerable. What if he'd gotten tired of waiting and left?

"Emma. Over here." And there he was, just as I'd pictured him, lolling on a blanket with an open book next to him. He was wearing khaki shorts and a polo shirt, looking just the same as always, but suddenly the sight of him made my stomach flip.

"Hi," I called, suddenly shy.

He was about thirty feet away. I picked a path through the people and blankets and picnic hampers.

"I wasn't sure you'd make it," Adam said as he closed his book and sat up. "I'm glad you did."

I hadn't expected him to be quite so magnanimous after our last prickly encounter. "I'm glad I got back in time."

"Did you have a good day?"

I nodded. "Yes." But I didn't offer any more information.

"Sit down," he said, an invitation, not an order. "Are you hungry?"

"You're always feeding me," I said, and the comment brought the sting of memory.

Even when we were grad students, Adam had indeed made a job out of keeping me supplied with sustenance. Pizza, Chinese takeout, popcorn for studying. The memories flooded back, and I was just tired enough to let them.

"I'm starving," I said, hoping to put myself on a more even keel with mundane conversation. "What have you got?"

It was surprisingly easy to forget about all that had happened over the past few days and simply enjoy Adam's company. I knew a more serious talk was coming. It had to. But he produced bread, cheese, and olives, and I was a lost cause.

Half an hour later, the orchestra began to play. Dusk fell, and eventually, the stars came out. The music went on and on. At some point, I leaned back, and Adam, seeing my exhaustion, offered me his chest to lean against.

"Thanks," I murmured, and not long after, I closed my eyes. The music, the darkness, and the sense of peace and safety conspired to lull me into the deepest sleep I'd had in weeks.

Sometime later, I woke up when I felt Adam's lips brushing the top of my head. "Hey, Em, it's time to go."

Startled, I sat up and looked around. Everyone was packing up their picnic baskets and folding their blankets.

"What time is it?"

"After ten," Adam answered. He stretched and rolled to his feet. "I didn't want to wake you, but I was pretty sure you wouldn't want to spend the night on the lawn."

I paused. By rights, he should have been furious with me. I should have been furious with him. But the evening had been a bit of the calm before the storm, and I didn't want to spoil it.

"What can I help with?" I asked, and Adam and I set about gathering the things he'd brought. As people faded off into the night, I knew that whatever might happen next, at least we'd had one blissful evening together.

☕☕☕☕☕

The conversation I'd been dreading started as we made our way home from Kenwood. Adam had brought Anne-Elise's car, so we didn't have to walk back to Hampstead in the dark. I followed him gratefully to the parking lot and climbed into the little Ford. Before he put the key in the ignition, he turned toward me.

"Em, it's time for us to be honest with each other."

"I don't know, we're doing so well at being dishonest, maybe we should just keep going."

He chuckled and smiled, as I'd hoped he would. "I wish that would work."

"You never know . . ."

"Yeah, you do."

I hated it when he was right. "Okay. I guess we might as well get it over with."

We both smiled in a rueful sort of way.

"Adam—"

"Me first." He paused. Then he reached out and took my hand. "Em, I'm sorry about what happened with Edward. I really am. I never liked him, but nobody deserves to be treated like he treated you."

I blinked back tears. "Thanks. And thank you for not saying, 'I told you so.'"

"You're welcome. But I did tell you."

"Yes, you did," I answered with a sad chuckle. "At least I can laugh about it now."

"That's something."

I drew a deep breath. The time had come to do what I'd shown up at Kenwood to accomplish. I just hadn't realized how very much it would hurt.

"Adam, it's been great seeing you here in London."

"That sounds ominous."

"It's just that, well, I've decided the only way for me to get past the past is to put all of it behind me."

"All of it? Meaning, what? Edward? Your job? Me?"

I nodded, although I had to force my neck to cooperate. "I need a fresh start. On my own."

"I wasn't aware I was keeping you from doing that." He dropped my hand.

"It's not you. It's me." The words didn't sound any less trite when I said them aloud than they had in my mind.

"For a woman who wanted to be a writer, that's a pretty clichéd excuse."

"Please don't be angry."

"Don't be angry? Man, Emma, you really are a piece of work."

I'd known this would be a painful undertaking, but still, it hurt even more than I'd imagined.

"I'm going to leave London in a day or two," I said. "Until then, maybe it would be better if we, I don't know, went our own ways." Then I wouldn't have to sneak out of the house or worry that he would follow me to Mrs. Parrot's. And I wouldn't be tempted to follow him to her house either.

"Emma—"

I held up a hand. "I don't see a lot of reason to drag this out. I've made my decision."

Adam flopped against the driver's seat. "You've taken me for granted just like always." He put his hands on the steering wheel. "As long as I've known you, our relationship has been all about you. Your love life. Your happy ending. Your angst over being good enough. And I've listened and supported and walked through all of it with you. Until Edward."

"And then because you didn't like him, you abandoned me." I jabbed back at him, because there was enough truth in his assertion to make me very uncomfortable.

"That's what you think? That I gave up on our friendship because I didn't like Edward?"

"It's true, isn't it?"

"Of course it's true. But if you think that was the reason, you're an idiot."

"I don't understand."

"No, you don't. You never did, Em. You never did."

"Adam—"

"The thing about obsessing about a happy ending, Emma, is that you forget to enjoy the journey along the way. You forget to appreciate the people alongside you."

"I always appreciated you."

"You appreciated my focusing on you, and when you fell for Edward, you made it clear you didn't need me anymore."

That one hit home. "I'm sorry. I know I got caught up in the moment—"

"No you didn't." He looked at me, his gaze piercing me like an arrow. "You made a clear choice, Em, between me and Edward."

"You just didn't approve because he was our adviser."

"I reiterate my assertion that you're an idiot."

"Adam—"

"Emma, do you not have sense enough to know when a man's in love with you?"

A single solitary pin dropping would have sounded like a cannon at that moment.

"You weren't—"

"Of course I was."

"But we were friends—"

"Your choice. Not mine. I wasn't brooding enough to be your Darcy, or condescending enough to be Mr. Knightley."

I didn't want to feel the surge of regret and shame that washed through me like the sea at high tide.

"Not once, until today, have you asked me what I'm doing in London. Really asked me about it, beyond the superficial," he said.

"You wouldn't have told me the truth." I bristled, thinking of Mrs. Parrot.

"How do you know? You never gave me the chance."

"Then why are you here in London?" I sounded like a petulant child, but I didn't care.

"I've been offered a job."

That was the last thing in the world I'd expected to hear. I clutched my hands together in my lap. "Where?"

"University of London. King's College."

"Oh." I had no idea what else to say. Finally, I summoned up a wobbly "Congratulations."

"I was doing something else, too, while I was here. Something to do with you."

"Me? You came to London for me?"

"No, but I received a strange phone call at Anne-Elise's house a couple of weeks ago. From a Mrs. Parrot. She said she was a friend of yours. She summoned me on a matter of life and death. Your life and death, at least figuratively speaking."

"A couple of weeks ago?"

"I don't know how she knew," Adam said. "Maybe she worked for MI5 or 6, or whatever they call it here, during the Cold War. But that woman could give lessons to the CIA in espionage."

"How she knew what?" My heart was pounding in my throat.

"How she knew how I felt about you. About our past. She must have a dossier on you three inches thick."

I swear that at that moment, time stood still. I know people are always saying that, and I've always thought it was an exaggeration, but right then I knew it to be true.

"But you and me . . . that was a long time ago." My voice was weak, just like my knees.

"For you, maybe." That was all he said. But it was enough to make me feel as if my lungs were being squeezed in my chest.

"Are you saying Mrs. Parrot has been meeting with you for romantic purposes?" I hadn't considered this sort of possibility at all.

"Yes. She's been counseling me, I guess you'd say. Helping me figure out how to get back in your life."

"So that's why you were—" I stopped myself just in time. I wasn't ready to tell Adam that I'd followed him two days before to South Kensington.

"At the theater? Yes. She called me after she gave you the tickets and asked if you'd invited me to go with you. When I said no, she told me to pick up the ticket she had for me at the box office and find you there. She didn't mention, though, that you'd be bringing a date."

"She didn't know about Barry." My head was spinning. "Adam, how did you know that she wasn't just some random crazy person?"

"Are you kidding? Don't you know who she is?"

I gave him what I'm sure was a blank look. "Who is she?"

He sighed. "Emma, what in the world have you been talking with her about on all these visits? Don't you know she's one of the greatest living experts on nineteenth-century British women writers?"

"That can't be. I've never heard of her in my life."

"Not under her current name, Parrot. No. She uses her first husband's name. You've heard of Gwendolyn Garnet-Jones."

It was a good thing I was sitting in the car seat. Gwendolyn Garnet-Jones was a world-renowned scholar. Many women in academia used the names they'd first published under as their professional names, but this was too much.

"You're kidding. I thought she was a recluse."

"She's not exactly hitting the conference circuit now, is she?"

"Why?" I shook my head. "Why would she care?"

"I suppose she had her own reasons." Adam shrugged.

It was all too much. "Adam, I want to go home."

"But we haven't finished—"

"Yes, we have." I steeled myself to do what was necessary. "I'm sorry Mrs. Parrot dragged you into this, and I appreciate how sweet you've been to me. But like I said, I'm ready to put the past in the past and move on."

"Just like that?"

I nodded, because I couldn't speak past the lump in my throat anymore.

"Fine." He was truly angry now. "Fine. You want it, Emma, you got it."

He thrust the gearshift into drive and took off across the parking lot. I held on for dear life.

"You're worth more than what you're settling for, Em," he said as we whizzed down the road toward Anne-Elise's house. "Much more."

But I'm not, I wanted to say. I guess I'd known that all along, and my weakness now simply proved it. I could blame my lack of a happy ending on Edward all day long, but the truth was that my own dissatisfaction with my life wasn't anybody's fault but mine. I'd been looking for a man to sweep me off my feet when I should have been looking for one who was willing to pick up the pieces. Not some fictional hero, but a real flesh-and-blood man. Someone who would love me for the long haul. Someone like Adam.

I didn't say anything more, just closed my eyes and prayed that we'd get to Anne-Elise's quickly, before I dissolved into a puddle right there in the car and told Adam the truth—that although I hadn't been in love with him all those years ago, I was most definitely in love with him now, and the idea terrified me more than if he'd turned over the steering wheel at that very moment and demanded that I drive on the wrong side of the road.

CHAPTER
TWENTY-THREE

*I*n November of 1802, a year after Jack Smith's death, Jane Austen accepted that now infamous marriage proposal from Harris Bigg-Wither, the brother of two of her closest friends. As the son of a landed family, Harris inherited a large fortune and a great deal of property. If Austen had married him, she would have lived in ease and comfort for the rest of her life. She would have been able to provide quite generously for her mother and sister. And she would have been completely, utterly miserable.

As Austen wrote in *Pride and Prejudice*, "Do anything rather than marry without affection." But even Austen's strong principles sometimes wavered.

The morning after she accepted the proposal, Austen withdrew her consent to the marriage. The consequent awkwardness and embarrassment led her to flee from Manydown, the Bigg-Withers' stately home in Hampshire. So Austen not only knew the agony of turning down an offer of marriage prompted by love, as she had with Jack Smith, but she had also experienced the enormous temptation of marrying for money without it.

⚜⚜⚜⚜

The morning after my fateful picnic with Adam, the skies opened and poured forth enough rain to launch a fleet of arks. I joined the throng of commuters tramping through the puddles on the streets of London. For the last time, I made my way to South Kensington and Mrs. Parrot's home on Stanhope Gardens.

"Come in out of the rain, my dear," Mrs. Parrot said, taking my wet umbrella from me and plunking it down into the elephant's-foot stand. "Let me take your jacket."

My old anorak had seen better days, but she treated it as if it were finest mink, placing it on a satin-padded hanger in the hall closet. Shame burned my cheeks. I couldn't remember ever having set out to deceive someone like this, and I couldn't allow myself to think about it or I would lose my nerve.

"So you've been to Chawton," she said as I followed her into the lounge. "How was your journey?"

"Fine." Guilt had my tongue in a vise.

"And were you able to complete your task?" She settled into her customary chair, and I took my place on the sofa at her left hand.

"Yes, but I'm not sure of its purpose." Touching a table was not exactly an endeavor worthy of Hercules.

"But I'm sure you felt it, didn't you, dear?"

"Felt it?"

She shook her head. "You're not a very good liar, Miss Grant. I can see it in your eyes that you sensed the presence there. The peace."

I sagged against the sofa cushions and nodded. "Yes. Yes, I did."

"And what did you think of her letter?"

"I thought it made everything quite clear."

"Yes, it does. Her wishes were explicit. She was afraid, rightly so, that because she was a woman, the minutiae of her life would be used to discredit her work. After all, look at what's happened to those poor Brontës."

"She must have trusted her sister a great deal." I couldn't imagine allowing myself to rely on someone like that, not after what had happened with Edward.

"She did, indeed, and as it turned out, her trust was well founded."

"When did Cassandra form the Formidables?" I kept my voice calm, not allowing the trembling in my limbs to infect it. I had this one last chance to gather information before I exposed Mrs. Parrot and her compatriots to the world.

"Near the end of her life, although she must have been cultivating her choices long before."

"And how did you come to be part of the group?"

She shook her head. "That's something we don't share with outsiders."

"Then how do you know someone is a bona-fide member? Couldn't just anyone turn up on your doorstep claiming to be a Formidable?"

Mrs. Parrot paused and pursed her lips, as if struggling with a decision. Finally, she said, "Very well. I can share this much with you. There are only a handful of us at any given time. Never more than five, certainly. We would know if someone was an impostor."

"So you and Miss Golightly and . . ." I trailed off in hopes that she would supply the other names, but I should have known better than to try such a ham-handed approach.

"That remains our secret," Mrs. Parrot said.

"Then why tell me?" I had asked her before but had never received a satisfactory answer. "Luring me here, interfering in my personal life—"

"It was your personal life, in addition to your professional credentials, that brought you to our notice," Mrs. Parrot said.

"But how could you know about Adam?" That was perhaps the most baffling question of all.

For the first time since we'd met, Mrs. Parrot looked uncomfortable. "I must confess to a bit of subterfuge. I called your cousin, that delightful Anne-Elise, some months ago and led her to believe that you were a candidate for a rather prestigious academic award." Mrs. Parrot coughed discreetly behind her hand. "She was very excited for you and most . . . forthcoming."

I groaned. Anne-Elise had never been known for her restraint. Especially not when it came to those she loved.

"And her invitation to stay? Adam and me at the same time? You put her up to that, I presume."

"Merely suggested, my dear. She saw at once the brilliance of the scheme."

"But why interfere in my romantic life too?"

Mrs. Parrot leaned over and patted my hand. "Because we needed you to feel what Jane had felt so that you could see the wisdom of our decision. Our life's work. A woman who has lost love, and then found it again, is precisely the kind of person we're looking for."

I sat there, mouth agape, no idea what to say. How in the world was I supposed to respond to these revelations?

"Now, we must address the business at hand," Mrs. Parrot said, clearly ready to proceed with her own agenda.

"The business at hand? I thought I was finished with the tasks."

"You are." She leaned forward and opened a file folder on the small table in front of us. "There they are." She nodded toward the papers it contained. "The originals of all the letters you have seen."

"Even the one that Miss Golightly had in Bath?" I looked up at her in surprise.

"Yes. Even that one."

"But how—"

"Please, my dear, whatever you do, don't take me for a fool. I know that you've already copied one of the letters, but I also know you haven't done anything about it. It's only to be expected, really. I bear you no ill will. And I suppose I wasn't quite truthful myself. There is a test after all."

"But you said—"

"The time has come for you to make your decision."

"My decision?"

"I'm going to leave the room in a moment." She tapped a finger against the top piece of paper. "There's a new letter there. Please read it, if you would. And then I've left you a short note underneath. After that, it's up to you."

"What's up to me?"

"Dear me, you do want it spelled out, don't you? Why, then it's up to you whether you honor your promise to me or not. If you decide to leave with the letters, I won't do anything to stop you."

I blanched. I knew that I did because I could feel all the blood drain from my cheeks. "I wouldn't—" But I couldn't finish the sentence. At least I still had enough integrity not to lie to her face.

"Begin with the letter on top," Mrs. Parrot reiterated as she rose to her feet. "I wish you well, Miss Grant. It's been many years since we've had someone come this far. I trust you will do justice to my faith in you." Were her eyes misty or simply bleary with age? "Good day."

I watched her hobble from the room, her distinctive orange hair not quite combed out in the back, revealing little white patches of scalp. The red flowered print of her dress clashed dreadfully with her hair. For all the eccentricities, I was truly going to miss Mrs. Parrot.

Of course, on the morning when I really could have used a cup of tea, she hadn't offered me one, so I was left to retrieve the letter that rested on top of the pile and read it without benefit of caffeine.

WINCHESTER, 15 JULY 1817

My dearest Cass,

You will think it strange I should write a letter when you are even now in the house, but I find my heart bears my words better on the page than on my lips. I assure you, in answer to your question of last night, I have been very happy to have had you as my life's companion. To be sure, as a girl, I longed for Henry Tilney, a boy of good family who would provide a little gothic romance before settling into respectability. In my youth, I hoped for the romance of a Mr. Darcy or even the adoring devotion of a Mr. Knightley. After Jack's death, I thought to find my Edward Ferrars, a quiet man of the cloth who would remain steadfast in the face of adversity. And now, at the end, I have learned I may only conjure on the page that hero I seek—the one death took from me so soon. Captain Wentworth is, of course, my own dear Jack, and by my pen, he lives still. Perhaps he will live forever, as I will not . . .

I had to stop because of the tears that filled my eyes.

. . . You asked me last evening if I regretted relenting to your persuasions against an imprudent marriage all those years ago. I will not allow you to take that burden upon your shoulders. My life has been my own, and I would not have lived it otherwise. I have loved as

bravely and sensibly as any woman may, given the stric-
tures of my heart and the flaws in my character.

Yrs always,

J. Austen

I set the letter on top of the others, but not before I slid an elegant piece of lavender writing paper from the pile. By now I recognized Mrs. Parrot's hand. I opened the paper, which had been folded into fourths, and began to read.

Dear Miss Grant,

On behalf of the Formidables, I extend this invita-
tion to you to join us in our endeavor. You have shown
both character and courage, and we would be delighted to
count you among our number.

Yours,

Gwendolyn Higginbotham Garnet-Jones Parrot

I couldn't have said which missive surprised me more.

❧❧❧❧❧

If I'd known how my marriage would end, would I have changed it? I wanted to say yes, that it hadn't been worth the pain and anguish, but I couldn't. If I had known, I might not have had the courage to love Edward. Like Austen, I had loved as bravely and as sensibly and as imperfectly as I could. That's what Jane Austen's letters had taught me. That attempting to know the future, to predict the outcome of love, would always negate the possibility of a happy ending.

Heartbreak is more common than happiness. No one wants to say that, but it's true. We're taught to believe not only that everyone deserves a happy ending, but also that if we try hard enough, we will get one. That's simply not the case. Happy endings, lifelong loves, are the products of both effort and luck. We can control them, to some extent, and though our feelings always seem to have a life of their own, we can at least be open to love. But luck, the other component, well, there's nothing we can do about that one. Call it God's plan or predestination or divine intervention, but we're all at its mercy. And sometimes God doesn't seem very merciful. Jane taught me that.

I looked down at the letters in my hands. Seven in all. A fraction of the treasure trove in the possession of the Formidables. But it would be enough, if I decided to stand up and walk out of Mrs. Parrot's house with them in my possession. They could be authenticated, I could write the definitive paper on the love of Jane Austen's life, and, like magic, my standing in the academic world would be restored. I could find a job, be invited to speak at conferences, spit in Edward's eye. Everything I'd wanted was there, literally in my grasp.

Or I could accept Mrs. Parrot's invitation and join her in keeping the greatest secret I would ever know, a task for which I was wholly unqualified, given that I'd had every intention of betraying the Formidables from the beginning. But for some reason, she trusted me, and that faith made all the difference.

With slow, careful movements, I smoothed the papers with my fingertips. And then just as carefully, I set them back on the table, both Austen's letters and the one from Mrs. Parrot. The pain that exploded in my chest almost brought me to my knees, but I knew that it was emotional, not physical. I pushed myself up from the sofa cushions, snagged my purse from the floor beside me, and lumbered toward the door of the lounge.

"Miss Grant?" I could hear Mrs. Parrot calling after me, but I didn't stop. Instead, I picked up speed, almost skidding across the tile floor of the foyer.

The door handle resisted my first attempt to wrench it open, but then it gave way. I flung the door open, stumbled down the steps, and hurled myself along Stanhope Gardens. Twenty feet along, I began to run. I ignored the curious glances and the invectives of the people I bumped against as I fled. I had to run, as quickly as possible, before I changed my mind. I was throwing it all away, stupidly, insanely.

Honorably.

Because, in the end, it wasn't Jane Austen's contagious predeliction for a happy ending that had contaminated my life. It was the sense of honor she'd instilled in me along the way. I could neither expose the Formidables nor join them, and I certainly couldn't ruin Jane Austen's life now, given all that she'd meant to mine.

I only stopped running when I'd reached the Underground station and realized I didn't have any idea where I was going. I needed time to think things over. I needed some caffeine, preferably a latte. And I needed to figure out what in the world I was going to do with my life now.

everal hours and two skinny vanilla lattes later, I called my parents and finally told them the truth about my marriage and why it had ended. Once they got over the initial shock, they were very supportive. The second call I made was to Anne-Elise's house.

"Meet me at Hatchards," I said when Adam answered the phone.

"What? Who is this?"

"It's Emma. Can you meet me at Hatchards bookshop? Now?"

I heard him take a deep breath, and I held my own.

"Emma—"

"Please, Adam. It's important."

"I thought you didn't want to see me anymore."

"It's not a matter of want. I need to explain something to you."

"I don't think—"

"Just this one last time, Adam. Then I won't ask for anything else."

A long silence. And then, finally, "All right. I can be there in an hour."

"I'll be waiting in the classics section."

After I hung up, I took several deep breaths before emerging from the phone booth. One hour to find the right words for the man I now realized I loved with all my heart.

No pressure.

With a strangled laugh, I set out in the direction of Hatchards.

❦❦❦❦❦

I was there, waiting for him when he arrived. I'd been skimming a copy of *Persuasion*, hoping to gain a little literary courage.

"Hey," he said.

He was out of breath, and that fact made my heart twist in my chest. A man who would hurry to meet you, even when you'd put him through what I'd put Adam through, was a man worth hanging on to. My heart banged against my ribs and anticipation set every nerve ending on fire.

"Hey." I couldn't make small talk. Not at a time like this. I said, in a rush of words, "I'm going back."

"You're going back to Edward?" Adam's face fell.

"No, back home. I'm moving back in with my parents."

"Oh." He looked at a complete loss. And then I could see

frustration and even a little anger as his mouth tightened. "You couldn't have told me that over the phone?"

I shook my head. "No."

He reached out, took my hand in his. His touch felt good and right, and I had to fight to keep from throwing myself in his arms. It would have been so easy to do that, to let him rescue me. To make the same mistake again.

"Emma, don't do this. You can stay here with me," he said, his gaze locked on mine. "You can marry me. We can make a new start. The university provides housing in the fall. I can probably find you a teaching position."

"But I'd be making the same mistake I made with Edward." I don't know how I managed it, but I pulled my hand free of his. "I'd be trying so hard to find the happy ending again that, as someone with a weird kind of wisdom once told me, I'd be missing out on the happy beginning."

"I love you, Em."

Last time, Edward had broken my heart for me, but this time, I was breaking it all by myself. "I love you too, Adam."

"This makes no sense."

"It does. Just not in the usual way."

"I still don't understand."

"I know. But Jane Austen would."

He looked up, as if appealing to God for some help. Actually, he probably was. "So if you still don't want to be with me, why did you ask me to come all the way down here to Hatchards?"

"I didn't say that I don't want to be with you. I said I can't be with you. Not yet." I paused, swallowed, clutched the copy of *Persuasion* in my hands. "I can't believe I'm saying this, but I need more time, Adam."

"A decade wasn't enough?" he said with a hoarse laugh.

"Apparently not." The fact that he wasn't whirling on one foot and stalking away was a testament to what a good man he was.

"How much time are we talking? A few weeks? A few months?"

"I have no idea."

He frowned, his face darkening. "Em, I can't wait around anymore to see if you'll someday decide it's okay for us to be together."

"I know. So I'm not asking you to." I thought of Jane Austen and her Jack. Yes, it would be wonderful if all love stories turned out like one of Austen's novels, but real life didn't work that way. Not my real life, anyway. Not Jane's, either.

"What will you do back in the States?"

"I talked to my parents before I called you. My dad thinks he can get me a teaching position at a local private school. And . . ." I paused, not sure whether to share the other part of my plan. But Adam deserved to know. "I'm going to start writing again."

The begrudging look of approval in his eyes gave me the boost of courage I needed so badly at that moment. "I know it's probably a pipe dream," I continued, "but I have to try. It may be too late, or I may not be any good at it, but it's a part of me, Adam. And I have to honor that, and see where it leads me."

My father would have said it was God's will. Jane Austen would have said that a novelist's heart couldn't be denied. But all I could say was that at long last, I had found the one thing that might put me on the right path. And I had Jane Austen, my parents, Adam, and maybe even some divine plan to thank for it.

"I owe you so much," I said, but he held up a hand in protest.

"You don't owe me anything, Em."

"I'm sorry this isn't the happy ending you wanted."

He flashed a small, tight smile. "Well, you never know. Maybe our story's not over yet."

Tears in my eyes, I returned his smile. "I hope not. I guess time will tell."

He reached for my hands again. "Do we have to keep avoiding each other until you leave?"

I shook my head. "No, although I wouldn't blame you if you wanted to chuck me under the nearest double-decker bus."

He paused as if considering the idea, and I laughed. "Adam—"

And then he squeezed my hand. "I just want you to be happy, Em. That's all I ever wanted. Well, almost all."

"Ditto," I said.

And then he kissed me for the second time, right there in

Hatchards, in front of the Brontës, Dickens, Shakespeare, and everybody.

And I knew that while the path I'd chosen wouldn't be easy, it would be okay. I had Jane Austen to thank for that.

Epilogue

In the end, I couldn't bring myself to visit Winchester, the Hampshire town where Jane Austen was laid to rest in the famous cathedral. I knew that her family had placed no mention of her writing on her monument, instead praising her for "the benevolence of her heart, the sweetness of her temper, and the extraordinary endowments of her mind." In fact, she was accorded the honor of burial in the cathedral not because of her novels but because of her family's ecclesiastical connections. She was the daughter, sister, and friend of clergymen.

She'd arrived in Winchester a short time before her death in hopes that a physician there could give her some relief from her suffering. Instead, she endured her final days far from the little cottage at Chawton, before at last finding the solace she must have craved. Modern scholars speculate that Austen suffered from Addison's disease, a failure of the adrenal glands thought to be the result of an infection. She died at the age of forty-one.

Two novels—*Northanger Abbey*, the first one she'd completed many years before, and *Persuasion*, her last—were not
published until after her death. For many years, her brother
Henry's short biographical sketch, published as a preface to the
two novels, was all that was known of her life.

After I fled Mrs. Parrot's house, I didn't want to think
of Austen as she had been at the end of her days—frail and
wracked by illness. I much preferred to remember the biting
wit of her letters, the magnificence of her novels, her courage
in the face of devastating loss, her devotion to her family. I left
England a few days after my last disastrous visit to Stanhope
Gardens. Adam and Anne-Elise went with me to the airport.
We stopped at a mailbox on the way so I could mail my letter
of apology to Mrs. Parrot. I wanted her to know, despite my
abrupt departure, how much I appreciated her faith in me.

On the flight home, my seatmate turned out to be an editor
from a New York publishing house. By the time we touched
down on American soil, she'd invited me to send her some
pages from the novel I was working on. Obviously, I didn't tell
her that there weren't any actual pages yet. I think Jane would
have approved.

My parents were waiting for me at the other end, and I was
grateful for their support. I had come full circle, but I also had
the chance to begin again. It was, in the most unexpected way,
the happiest beginning I could have imagined.

Author's Confessions

As far as I know, the character of Jack Smith is fictional, as are Mrs. Parrot and the Formidables. The wardens of St. Nicholas Church, Steventon, don't still keep the key inside the yew tree, and with apologies to the house of Chanel, no such dress as I described exists. These elements are all poetic license on my part.

What is true are the basic facts of Jane Austen's life. She was one of eight children of an Anglican clergyman, her family supported her in her writing endeavors, her novels were published anonymously, and she never married. She did make those entries in the parish register, but as far as we know, they were a girlish prank. Her father did indeed take in pupils to educate alongside his own sons, and not all of their names are known. Other than the small, half-finished watercolor by her sister, Cassandra, no formal portraits of Austen exist.

In later years, Cassandra did speak to a niece about a man

whom Jane had met at the seaside, a man whom she greatly admired and hoped to see more of, but he died before they could pursue their acquaintance further. And Cassandra did, as far as we know, destroy the bulk of her sister's letters before her death.

Jane Austen's circumscribed country life and her sister's censorship have kept her a rather veiled literary figure. For many years, biographers and scholars, beginning with her great nephew James Austen-Leigh, presented her as a quiet, reserved, proper woman, but one has only to read her novels to realize that she was nothing so bland. Her genius, her craft, and her timeless prose are no secret, but thanks to Cassandra's scissors, most other aspects of her life will probably remain a mystery. I can only hope that her admirers, of which I am but one of many, may be forgiven for their speculations, and that this novel, and others related to Jane Austen, will promote a continued interest in her life and her work.

Beth Pattillo
February 2009

Reading Group Guide

1. Emma Grant, the main character, has always believed she deserved a happy ending; in fact, she thinks that Jane Austen promised her one. Do you think our culture promotes this ideal too much? Why or why not? What is your definition of a happy ending? Do you think this book has a happy ending?

2. What do you think of Emma's choice to return home and begin again, rather than to remain in England? If you were in her shoes, what do you think you would have done?

3. Emma and Jane Austen are both the daughters of clergymen. How do you think that influenced them? Give examples from this novel or from one of Jane Austen's novels.

4. In some ways, Jane Austen conformed to the standards of her time and in others she defied convention. Do you believe that men and women should be held to different standards of behavior? Why or why not?

5. Were the Formidables right to keep Jane Austen's letters a secret? What would you have done in their position?

6. Emma's father taught her that God had a plan for her life. Do you believe this is true? If so, how specific is God's plan? How much choice do we have in the matter? If not, do you believe that life is a matter of random choices and consequences? What led you to this belief?